The Mountain Chronicles

For The Strength of The Hills

Based On A True Story

The Mountain Christians

For The Strength of The Hills

Based On A True Story

LUX LUCET IN TENEBRIS

A LIGHT SHINES IN THE DARKNESS

Hiram J. Bertoch

The Mountain Christians

For The Strength of The Hills

Editor: Alesha Goble || Editor: Karrie Robison

Cover art by Cindy Grant || Cover Design By F. Wiggen

Expert Reader: Annie Hedberg

Photography: Leah-Anne Thompson || Photography: Strokket

www.MountainChristians.com

Library of Congress Control Number: 2012920206

Copyright © 2013 Piedmont Pages Imprint

10 9 8 7 6 5 4 3 2 1

ISBN: 978-0-9845736-6-0

ISBN: 0-9845736-6-6

Imprint: Piedmont Pages

Hunter, Utah

To Those Many

Local Mentors Who Set An

Example For Me of What

True Manhood Is.

Scout Leaders, Bishops, Neighbors,

Young Men's Presidents...

Who Love Their Wives, Treasure Their Children,

And Who Enjoy Working Hard!

Contents

1849

Chapter One

From the Mountains of Deseret

"Try these potatoes, Joseph, they are excellent."

After being confined to a ship for nearly two months, Lorenzo was more grateful than ever for the Lord's bountiful blessings; good food being at the top of that list. Lorenzo smiled broadly as he pushed a small wooden bowl across the table toward his traveling companion.

The journey from Salt Lake City to London, England, had been relatively uneventful. He and Joseph Toronto had spent most of their slow, tedious voyage making plans and seeking guidance from the Lord. Brigham Young had asked the two men to travel to Italy, and as he had put it, "Wherever else the Lord would lead you, to open those areas up to the gospel."

It had been a very difficult assignment for both men to accept. The memory of having been chased out of Nauvoo by the cowardice of an unrelenting and dangerous mob was still at the forefront of their minds. After narrowly escaping the grasp of these wild men, Lorenzo and Joseph then had to walk with their wives and children for months across a dusty and unforgiving wilderness.

Then finally, after having endured the most extreme limits of physical exhaustion, sickness, and mental and emotional fatigue, they had arrived in the mountain valley in a land that Brother Brigham called Deseret. Here, he had told them, they would build their new homes. A place where, after years of abuse from persecutors, they could now find security. Protected by the strength of the majestic Rocky Mountains, their children and grandchildren would at last be safe. And here Brother Brigham assured them, they would live in peace for generations to come.

But Lorenzo Snow and his companion, Joseph Toronto, would not get to enjoy their new city for long. They had scarcely begun to build their homes and plant their crops, when the call to meet with the Prophet had come.

On the appointed day, Lorenzo and Joseph met outside the cabin that had been erected for the Young family. After exchanging nervous greetings, they entered Brother Brigham's home together.

Brigham Young welcomed them with a broad smile and a firm handshake. He gestured them towards a bench along one of the cabin walls. He himself stood along the opposite wall by a large window, and began to speak.

"Brethren, the continent of Europe has long laid in apostasy," Brother Brigham glanced out the window at the patchwork of fields that were starting to take on the appearance of a town. He continued looking back at them, "Some of us are called to remain here and build Zion, her streets, her homes, and her factories. And some of us are called of the Lord to travel abroad and find her future inhabitants."

"The Lord would like the two of you to travel together as companions to Europe. Once there, you are to establish his kingdom in that land."

To Lorenzo, it had been a daunting request. For any man,

let alone a couple of humble and under-educated farmers, to be expected to stand in Europe among the great aristocrats and command enough respect to find converts, it was almost unthinkable.

Even if they could somehow manage to find an audience willing to listen to their message, the chances of anyone converting seemed unlikely. Europe was a land that had been dominated by the Catholic Church for centuries. A faith that was deeply woven into every fiber of their society.

To say that Lorenzo had felt overwhelmed would have been an understatement. But he supposed that success in Europe was possible. After all, a few years earlier, John Taylor had fulfilled a mission to the British Isles. His efforts there had been a resounding success, and as a result, thousands had been brought to the knowledge of the restored gospel, including, in some cases, entire congregations. But they had been Protestants, not Catholics. Had the Lord prepared similar groups of people in Catholic Europe?

"Begin your mission in Italy, and from there go wherever the Spirit guides you." Lorenzo Snow and Joseph Toronto had been given no more guidance than this. They had not been told where in Italy to begin, or how the Lord expected them to go about fulfilling their assignment.

They returned home, kissed their young families goodbye, and leaving unfinished homes and unplanted farms behind, set out on their arduous journey towards Italy. After months of travel, Lorenzo and Joseph had at last arrived in London where they had remained for the past two weeks. Since arriving they had worked to learn as much as they could about the missionary work that had already been organized in England. Before continuing on to Italy, Lorenzo and Joseph had decided that it would be wise to find out as much as they could about the success that Brother Taylor had seen.

While in London, Lorenzo and Joseph had become acquainted with one Thomas Stenhouse, a newly converted Saint who was on fire with the gospel. Thomas had proven to be an energetic man, who was excited to do whatever he could to help Lorenzo and Joseph during their brief stop in London.

Tonight, like most of the other evenings they had spent in the British capital, Lorenzo and Joseph were dining in the Stenhouse home. Thomas' wife Elizabeth was a kindly, albeit shy woman. She was as passionate about the new Mormon religion as was Thomas, but unsure of herself when it came to expressing these feelings.

Thomas and Elizabeth had two young sons. The oldest was a six year old little gentleman named Micheal. He was the pride of his father, who unabashedly doted on him. Micheal eagerly returning that affection to his father. The younger son was a chubby toddler named Richard.

Lorenzo had come to love and admire Thomas. He was not afraid to get on the floor and wrestle with his sons, as some of the upper class men were. Lorenzo supposed that this was one of the blessings of being a part of the working class. Thomas earned enough money to provide for his family's needs, but he did not have to put on airs as he would have to have done if he had been born to a more noble family. They were free to simply be themselves.

"My dear Mrs. Stenhouse, once again you have outdone yourself! This pork is truly heaven sent!" pronounced Lorenzo, as Thomas' wife blushed. "Now, Thomas, I have something to discuss with you before we leave. Do you mind if we move into the drawing room?"

The Stenhouses lived in a small cottage just outside of

London. It was not fancy or extravagant, but like most homes in the area, it did have a small drawing room wherein guests could be entertained. In the center of this small room a few small couches had been positioned with their backs to one another. Along the walls, ornate wooden chairs had been placed underneath paintings of various Stenhouse ancestors. Between these chairs there stood handmade shelves. They were old but had been well cared for. These shelves were heavily laden and overflowing with a number of different nicknacks. Lorenzo supposed it likely that these items had been collected over several generations by the same people whose pictures now hung in reverence along the walls.

Thomas sat down on one of the wooden chairs along the wall. He gestured for Lorenzo and Joseph to take a seat, side by side, on one of the couches opposite himself. Once they were all seated, Lorenzo Snow began to speak, "Thomas, as you know, Joseph and I have been sent by the Prophet Brigham Young to do a great work on the European continent. And, as you also know, we have been seeking God's guidance in how we should proceed."

Thomas nodded.

"As I have inquired of the Lord's will, I have felt impressed, Thomas, that he would have you travel along with Joseph and I."

Lorenzo paused to make sure that Thomas understood him.

"If you will accept the Lord's call, then together, the three of us will enter Europe and, like Ammon and his brothers, we will bring the gospel to a land that has long been over-shadowed in apostasy. Together we will bring them the light of the gospel."

Thomas' face, which usually had a reddish tint to it, now appeared as pale as the full moon. He looked as white as someone recovering from a serious illness. Lorenzo wondered if perhaps this calling was too much for him. Maybe he should have selected his words more carefully, or prepared Thomas more thoroughly before issuing the call.

After a few moments of silence, Thomas' rosy color returned, and tears began to roll down his cheeks. Struggling to speak, Thomas looked at his dearly loved wife and asked for her opinion. "You have always been wise, my dear. What do you think I should do?"

Without even the briefest moment of hesitation, she answered, "Thomas, if the Lord is calling you, then you must go. We will be well enough off while you are gone."

ℰℷ

"See, Thomas, look here, this is it! This is where we will start." Nearly two months had passed since Lorenzo had called him to serve as a missionary in Italy. With each passing day, Thomas grew both more eager for the day of their departure, and also more concerned at the thought of leaving his family behind. He would miss his dear wife and tender children, but the privilege of serving the Lord, like Paul of old, filled Thomas with tremendous joy. And now, after a great deal of preparation and planning, they were just a few days away from their departure.

"Where?" Thomas didn't mean to sound so surprised, but he had not expected that they would begin their proselyting in such an unlikely place as Elder Snow was now showing him. Thomas had imagined that they would begin in one of the great Italian cities, perhaps Rome, or Sicily.

"The Alps?! Lorenzo, are you certain?" Thomas asked.

Thomas Stenhouse hadn't known Lorenzo very long. But since he and Joseph arrived from Salt Lake City two and a half months earlier, the three men had spent nearly all of their time together.

Lorenzo Snow was neither a young man, nor at the age of thirty four was he terribly old. And yet, despite lacking wrinkles, or having the ends of his hair dipped in gray, all qualities that tended to engender trust, he seemed to Thomas to be extraordinary. Though he had what Thomas would describe as relatively youthful features, Lorenzo also possessed something that, nevertheless, transcended age. A profound wisdom. An innate sense of what was right and what was wrong. So much so, that when he suggested that the three of them begin their mission by hiking to the top of the Italian Alps, where only the most experienced mountain climber would ever think to venture, Thomas did not hesitate for more than a few moments.

"If you believe that this is where the Lord wants us to go, Brother Snow, then we will travel to the top of these mountains," replied Thomas. "But," paused Thomas, "does anyone live there?"

"Indeed," said Lorenzo, as he pulled out a tattered, folded up map from his coat pocket. The map had been taken from a pamphlet printed just a few years earlier in 1846 by a group that called themselves *The Religious Tract Society*.

"There are three small valleys," Lorenzo explained, "known by those who live there as the Piedmont Valleys. And nestled within them is an ancient group of Christians that call themselves the Waldensians."

"Ah, yes!" Joseph chimed in. "I grew up hearing stories about them."

Joseph Toronto had been born and raised in Sicily, where he had spent most of his life. He had been converted to Mormonism a few years earlier after moving to the United States. Once there, Joseph had joined the body of Saints in Nauvoo.

"My family had believed them to be a stubborn and heretical people, who had long since lost their way from the grace of Rome," Joseph smiled.

Lorenzo chuckled. "The Waldensians have existed in these valleys for hundreds of years, completely separated from any other church. They predate even the Reformation. Many, including myself, believe that their religion extends all the way back to the original church established by Christ. The Waldensians indeed may have a stronger claim than the Catholics on who apostatized from the gospel first," Lorenzo said.

"Joseph, Thomas, the Lord has a work for us there. He has preserved them for centuries. Don't you think it is time that they be brought the good news of the restoration of the fullness of the gospel?" asked Lorenzo.

September 1849 – July 1850

Chapter Two

Lux Lucet in Tenebris

"Come here, my boy!"

James loved it when Papa referred to him as "my boy." Mama had died when he was only seven months old. James was the youngest of five children, and felt all the closer to his Papa as a result. Even though James could not remember Mama, he could tell that Papa missed her profoundly, and in a way, this made James miss her, too.

After Mama's death, Papa had worked hard to insure that James was raised properly. He had devoted all his energy to making certain that James grew up appreciating and loving his

Waldensian heritage. This additional attention only further deepened the close bond that existed between James and Papa.

James' four older siblings, two brothers and two sisters, had also pitched in to help raise him. James both loved and also detested being the youngest. He enjoyed the closeness he had with most members of his family. But he did not appreciate being frequently lectured by each of them when he made some unintentional mistake. It was as though each felt that it was their responsibility to correct his every action; his occasional follies often resulting in multiple lectures, one from each member of his family.

Raising James had been a family project. He enjoyed learning the various crafts that each had mastered. Though this sometimes also led to frustration. They were so far ahead of him, to James, it seemed that he would never be able to catch up. How could he ever learn to be as smart as Jean was? Or grow as strong as Daniel? And he couldn't imagine how he would master the art of singing beautiful music as well as Antoinette had.

"James, my boy, come here, son," Papa called.

James carefully climbed down from the stone wall that ran along a thin dirt lane; the purpose of the wall being to separate travelers from the heights below. This lane traversed the alpine wilderness and ultimately led to the family's similarly stone-clad mountain cottage. A beautiful little home surrounded by the last of autumn's wildflowers, which would soon all be covered in snow.

James set down the basket that he had been using to gather chestnuts from the trees that grew along the mountain crest, and looked up at Papa. He was a large, strong man, taller than most of the neighbors. Although he was getting on in years, James was proud knowing that his Papa could beat anyone in a wrestling match if he had to.

"Son, along with these chestnuts, I need you to also carry some potatoes to market. Drop them off on your way to subsidiary."

"Yes, Papa," James answered obediently, albeit in a disappointed tone of voice. He enjoyed picking chestnuts, but he did not care for subsidiary, nor did he look forward to the long, laborious walk between here and there. Now that he was ten years old, it was his responsibility to attend, and he was not about to disappoint his family, nor was he going to give any of them an opportunity to reprimand him again.

He placed the bag of potatoes over his shoulder, securing it with one hand, picked up his basket of chestnuts with the other, and began the long walk down the mountain trail.

As he made his way to the valley floor, James thought about what had happened a few months earlier when he had not been so wise in controlling his disappointment at having to make the daily trek to subsidiary.

"I don't want to go to subsidiary!" he'd said. "I want to stay here and help you and Papa."

James' oldest brother Jean was 24. He was a gentle man, who was patient, kind, and quietly intelligent. Some thought he was shy. But it wasn't shyness that tempered his mannerisms. Jean only spoke when it made sense to do so. He was comfortable with who he was. If there was something that needed to be said, Jean was not afraid to say it. Otherwise he kept his thoughts to himself.

"And you would be a fine helper, James! You are such a hard worker! You make us all proud," encouraged Jean. "But if you do not go to subsidiary, how ever will you learn to read?" Jean smiled as he continued to pursue the same line of reasoning. "And if you can't read, how will you learn to memorize the scriptures?"

Memorizing the scriptures was as important to the Waldensian people as was learning to walk or to hunt. James had been taught that beginning in the days of the apostles long ago, his people had been charged with this important task. It was a responsibility that God himself had appointed to them, and a task that generations of Waldensians had dedicated their lives to achieving, thus preserving the light of the scriptures for the rest of the world.

Jean continued teasing, "Do you want to be the first Waldensian in a thousand years who cannot recite the New Testament?" He began to tickle James. "Besides," Jean continued, "subsidiary only lasts for four months out of the year. You can endure that, James!"

The message was tender, but clear. You have a duty to your people, to your family, to yourself, and most importantly, to God. Yes, we are a community of farmers, who survives off the land, but each of us has a responsibility to learn the scriptures, and none of us must shirk in this duty.

Papa had frequently expressed his love for the scriptures to James. He had a way with words, and was a master storyteller. It was not uncommon for the family to gather around Papa and listen as he recounted from memory one of the great epic adventures recorded in the Bible. If the scriptures were important to Papa, then James knew that they should also matter to himself.

Each morning was essentially the same. James would begin his day by collecting chestnuts, or later when the season grew late and the chestnuts had all fallen from their barren branches, Papa would give James some other item, such as potatoes from storage, or wool to carry. These goods James would carefully haul down the steep, craggy path to the markets located on the valley floor below.

Long ago, James' people had been chased into these mountains by persecutors who had sought to take away their lives. Most of the Waldensians now occupied a region around three alpine valleys.

The valley floors served as a public gathering place, where temples, schools, libraries, and a few shops had been built. These valleys were themselves tucked away high in the Italian Alps, creating a natural fortress that could only be reached by scaling dangerous and difficult paths.

As James hiked toward the valley floor, he subconsciously reached out for a tree branch to steady himself, passing over and around boulders. It was a habit that all the people of the mountains acquired almost as early as they learned to walk. When one lives on a rugged mountainside, one has to learn how to hop from rock to rock without falling.

As James continued down the mountainside, he imagined the great battles that had taken place across the valleys over the centuries. In his mind he could see the heroes who had defended his people against the armies of the French, and the armies of the House of Savoy from the Kingdom of Sardinia. Sometimes only one of these militias advancing. Other times, both armies attacking simultaneously.

James had been taught that it was God who had persevered their people from destruction, and that despite the ceaseless attempts by powerful outside forces to obliterate the Waldensians, they continued to thrive in their valleys, because they had been chosen to preserve the gospel down through the centuries. Whilst the rest of the world had become burdened under confusion and apostasy, the people of the valleys continued to preach and practice the pure doctrine of Christ. Long ago, the rest of Christianity had united under a single bishop, who had taken upon himself the title of "Pope." But the Waldensians had remained apart. Their refusal to unite themselves to the religion that had then spread throughout Europe led to their suffering severe persecutions; many of their forefathers having suffered as martyrs for their faith.

The Waldensians were rounded up and hemmed in on all

sides, facing complete annihilation, unless they rejected their faith, and converted to the religion that the rest of Europe had accepted.

It was then that they discovered their beloved valleys. Retreating here, to the safety of the mountains, they were able to not only survive, but in time, to thrive, in a region that was uninhabitable such that no one else wanted it. These secluded mountain tops so treacherous that it proved too difficult for their persecutors to follow in any great number.

Here, wrapped in the protective strength of the mountains, James' people remained free from outside influences, where they could practice their faith, undisturbed by outsiders. Christianity could then be passed down from father to son for countless generations. The most important thing that they had preserved was, of course, a knowledge of the Holy Scriptures. For hundreds of years throughout the rest of Europe, reading the scriptures had become a forbidden activity. For lay persons who did not belong to the priestly order to be found possessing even a single of the Bible's pages could be cause for being put to death. But not here in the Piedmont Valleys. The people of the mountains not only owned copies of biblical passages, they memorized them. There was not a man or woman among them that could not recite vast portions of scripture from memory. After caring for their animals and tending their farms, their duty to God occupied most of their remaining time.

James had been taught that they stood as a light in the tops of the mountains. Indeed, the scriptures talked about such lights. Standing out in darkness, shining forth, giving light to the rest of the world. In their case, they literally were located in the tops of the mountains. The first thing Papa made James memorize was the Waldensian motto: "In darkness, light." Belonging to such a noble people made James stand tall.

Each morning, after what seemed to James to be hours of endless and arduous walking, he would eventually reach the valley floor. Completely exhausted from his journey, James would then make his way to the market square, where he would trade his meager goods for those items that his family needed that day, such as a bit of cloth or thread for his sister Marguerite, or a small piece of iron which Daniel could then use to fashion arrow tips for his bow. James would then make his way toward the schoolhouse. At the end of the day he returned home, his load blessedly lighter than it had been in the morning.

Upon entering their small stone home each evening, James

would eat a scanty meal before collapsing into his small bed, which he shared with his brothers. He would then wake the next morning, only to repeat the same dreary tasks all over again. A routine that continued until the winter snows grew too deep to allow the boys his age to attend subsidiary. They would then all retreat to their various homes, where they would remain, bundled in isolation, until the next spring, when the sun's warmth would in time begin to melt the snow. Then, like brown bears, slowly arising from their long winter hibernation, the people of the valleys would once again open their doors and, peaking their heads out, check to see if winter had relented sufficiently to allow them to carry on with their lives. At first only a few mountaineers ventured out, then in time a few more, until once again, the mountain became alive with activity. Everyone picking up life right where they had left off. Lovers, who by heavy snow had been kept from one another, could again embrace. Shopkeepers once again opened their stores. And on Sunday, the people could again return to temple services.

Blessed Sunday, a day of rest. The day that the Lord himself had set aside for mankind to sit outside under an open blue sky, and eat chestnuts, or take long naps. After their temple meetings were over, James would have the rest of the day to spend with his friends.

As winter faded and spring began to creep across the mountainside James and his friends spent Sunday afternoons throwing snow at each other, or digging out snow caves. As the snow melted, a process that often took many months, they moved on to other activities, such as hiking along the upper rim, teasing the mountain chamois as they pranced from ledge to ledge, or following the eagles as they soared over the rocky precipices.

At length, summer arrived, allowing the children of the valleys to divert themselves by playing endless rounds of capture the cattle, a game where one boy would play the role of the farmer, while the rest would act like escaped cattle doing their best not to get caught.

In late July, as James and his family traversed the rocky pathway toward temple, James' mind was not centered on the gospel as it probably should have been, but was instead occupied by thoughts of what he and his friends would do that afternoon.

Each of the three valleys had a number of small temples that had been built beginning in the mid 1500s. Prior to the existence of these little houses of worship, the Waldensians had supplicated their God outside under the sky or, during colder months, in their homes.

These temples were basic in structure. Built by stacking stones one on top of the other, they consisted usually of just a few rooms, including a small chapel, and a few other quarters where other business could be conducted. To an outsider, these buildings would appear to have been rather small, plain, and simple. They did not have stained glass windows, paintings, ornate crosses, or other such items. The Waldensians avoided these decorations, both due to their extreme poverty, which did not allow them the funds to purchase such things, and also out of a fear that the worship of images might enter into their church, as it had entered into other sects of Christianity.

As James and his family arrived at the little stone church house, they were met at the temple door by Barba Peyrot.

The commission of barba was a position of great respect. The title itself meaning "uncle," which reminded the people of how they were to treat these traveling pastors. Each had taken a vow of poverty, and had dedicated their lives to the work of the Lord. To that end, they visited the various temples around the valleys preaching sermons. In addition to preaching locally, they also visited other distant lands, serving as missionaries.

James often wondered what it would be like to leave the protection of their mountains and travel out into the world as a missionary. It was a tradition that a newly ordained barba would spend his first two years on a mission outside of the valleys. During this period they would preach the gospel, and help care for those who were ill or infirm. After returning to the valleys, the young barba then began his lifelong ministry in the service of the Lord. He would from then on be known as a "perfect" by the rest of the inhabitants of the valleys.

"Ah, Jean." Barba Peyrot took Papa by the arm with one hand and placed his other hand firmly on Papa's shoulder. "Jean, it is good to see you," he continued, as he looked Papa squarely in the eyes, smiling widely.

One of the primary responsibilities that the barbes bore was to make sure that all the people of the valleys were looked after. Ever since Mama's death, the barbes had paid particular attention to Papa and his little family.

Papa was, after all, sixty years old. An age that many did not reach in a place where life was spent in the midst of hard labor from birth until death.

Papa's two oldest sons, Jean, who had been named after him, and Daniel, were both strong and hardworking men. But the barbes were nevertheless faithful in their duty, insuring that this old widower and his children were frequently tended to. Or, rather, they did the best that they could. Unfortunately, there really wasn't any excess in the valleys, especially this year.

The mountain was in the middle of a blight, which had caused much of the spring harvest to fail. As a result, everyone was hungry to some extent or another. If the barbes did manage to find an extra bit of food, or procure some needed item, they would then distribute these scanty goods among the needy.

The extra attention that the barbes paid to his family meant that James knew many of them on a first name basis. Barba Peyrot was one of James' favorites. He was an older man, though not as old as Papa. Barba Peyrot wore a coarse robe, which had been donated to him from the people of the valleys who referred to themselves as "the friends of the perfect." What endeared Barba Peyrot to James was his kind face. Barba Peyrot always smiled, always looked directly in James' eyes, and made him feel as though he were important.

This occasion was no different. As he and Papa discussed

the meeting that was about to commence, Barba Peyrot looked down at James and said "James, today we have some guests who are going to preach to us. These travelers have come to us all the way from America." He smiled and asked James, "Young man, how do we treat visitors?"

James was hesitant to respond. He knew he was supposed to be respectful, but he wasn't sure about visitors from America. Nor did he understand why the barbes would allow anyone from so far away to preach in their temple. James had been taught that it was the responsibility of the people of the valleys to go out to the rest of the world to share the light of their gospel message. How could a visitor from America have anything to share with the people who inhabited the valleys?

Despite this confusion, James ventured a response, "we are err . . . respectful?" he replied. His tone of voice more asking than answering.

Barba Peyrot slapped him on the shoulder with delight, not detecting the uncertainty in his voice. "That is right, James! A fine young lad you have raised, Jean! Good young lad!"

Feeling relieved at having correctly answered the barba's inquiry, James walked proudly toward his seat. Papa kissed

Antoinette and Marguerite on their foreheads and ushered them across the room. James' sisters sat down with the rest of the women on the left side of the temple chapel, while the men sat on the right side.

James' earlier concern still perplexed him. "Papa," he asked. "Why did the barbes invite preachers from outside of the valleys to give us a sermon? I thought it was our job to bring the gospel to them."

Papa looked down at his boy with tremendous pride. "Yes, my boy," he gently answered, "you are correct. It is indeed our duty to bring the gospel and the scriptures to all the world. But this does not mean that we cannot listen to and learn from others."

"Son," he paused, "God has used our people to preserve the scriptures and the light of the gospel, this is true, but he has used others as well who also have important pieces of the gospel puzzle."

The gospel is a puzzle? wondered James. And God has used more than one people to preserve different pieces of it? James was pretty sure that not too many other Waldensians would have agreed with Papa on this.

James knew about the Great Apostasy; that the original church Christ had established had fallen into a variety of false beliefs, and that ultimately the people had been deprived of even the right to read the scriptures. Everywhere except, of course, here in the valleys where the right to freely read the scriptures had been preserved and, for that matter, the expectation to memorize them strongly encouraged.

James had also been taught that the Waldensians had close friends among those of the Reformation who had reached out to them beginning in the mid 1500s, and that together, the people of the valleys and the people of the Reformation had mutually enlightened each other.

But to invite preachers from America here! Into God's mountain tops and valleys? The sacred lands where the gospel had been preserved by the hand of the Lord himself? What could preachers from outside the valleys possibly know about the gospel?

However absurd the notion was that these American preachers would share anything that the perfects didn't already know, James was determined to be respectful. He was not about to let Barba Peyrot down.

The next hour was a difficult one for the ten year old James to endure. He did his very best not to let any trace of amusement or disbelief color his expressions, though both of these emotions occupied his heart. He was grateful that neither Papa nor Barba Peyrot were looking at him when the American preacher, who was introduced as Lorenzo Snow, had held up a book and claimed that it contained more scriptures in addition to the sacred Bible.

At this absurd pronouncement, James could not help but contort his face into a look of utter embarrassment for the poor fool. Any member of the temple congregation could have told the misguided man that there were no more scriptures besides those found in the Bible. They were, after all, the people who had spent generations protecting that sacred book. No one in the world knew her passages better than they did.

Poor man. Traveling from some distant land with the false notion that there were more scriptures to tell the world about, only to wind up in the heart of our mountains. The very place where the scriptures had always been protected. He would have been much better off if he had gone to some other land. At least there he might have found a people uneducated enough to believe him.

James looked up at Papa, expecting to see a similar expression on his face. However, he was surprised at what he saw. It was not an expression of embarrassment for the man, nor one of incredulity, as that which a few other faces around the room wore.

Instead, Papa had an expression of kind consideration.

Did Papa think the man might be right? Did Papa think that there indeed could be more scriptures other than those found in the Bible? James quickly pushed this ridiculous notion aside. No, James knew better. Papa was simply being polite.

James promptly removed the expression of embarrassment from his own face. Grabbing hold of Papa's hand, he resolved with renewed firmness to be as respectful as was his Papa. These preachers might not know what they were talking about, but James would not use that as an excuse to be rude to them.

After the meeting, the family made their way back to their home. As they walked, James held the hand of his Papa, beaming with pride. Many others in the meeting had been rude to the preachers. Not so much through unkind words, but rather through their body language. But not his Papa. His Papa had shown the utmost respect. James thought his Papa was the wisest man in the valleys.

"Did you hear what that preacher said?" giggled Marguerite.

At seventeen years of age, Marguerite was both the prettiest and also the silliest of James' sisters. Despite the overwhelming poverty that persisted in the valleys, Marguerite had somehow always managed to decorate herself with various forms of vanity. Whether it be a piece of old cloth cut and repurposed into a ribbon, or the feathers from one of the many eagles that inhabited their mountain tops placed carefully in her hair. Today she was sporting a simple bonnet that had been sewn at home using a coarse fabric spun from sheep's wool. But unlike most of the other young ladies her age, her bonnet was adorned with a couple of bright and colorful wildflowers. In addition to this, she had also added a small piece of silk to her ensemble which she had draped across her shoulders. Silk was one luxury that the Waldensian people enjoyed in small quantities. Not because they could afford such precious materials, but because their mountain tops were populated with a variety of mulberry trees. These trees attracted silk worms in great quantities. The worms gorged themselves on the natural mulberries and then left behind their silk cocoons, a present, which the Waldensian people could then spin into a fine and precious cloth. This silk was used primarily to create veils, which the women often wore in their temple meetings. But today, Marguerite had chosen to use a small piece to enliven her apparel.

"I don't know about scripture," commented Jean quietly.

"But did you see how new and pristine that book looked?" asked Jean. "I wish we could have gotten a closer look at it," he finished, as he looked toward Papa with an uncertain smile.

"Get a closer look at it!" laughed Marguerite, getting more boisterous the longer she went on. "Jean, don't be thick," she paused and smiled slyly. "His friend was very handsome, though. Don't you think, Antoinette?"

Marguerite smiled and glanced at Antoinette, who did not seem to appreciate the comment, nor did she acknowledge that it had been made. Marguerite enjoyed teasing her older sister, especially on matters of the heart.

Antoinette was a very different type of person from her younger sister Marguerite. Wherein Marguerite there was self-promotion and an eagerness to be the center of attention, in Antoinette there was a humble shyness and a willingness to stand unnoticed in the background. Antoinette was not as pretty as Marguerite, and this suited her just fine. She was not by any means homely. Plenty of suitors would have been attracted to her – had they known she existed. But few indeed knew that the widely admired Marguerite had an older sister.

James loved both his sisters, but he liked Antoinette the

most. Marguerite could be a friend at times, when it suited her. But she could just as quickly turn against you. Not Antoinette. She was loyal and gentle. Antoinette was the angel who had kissed James' forehead so many nights, or placed her cheek next to his and told him that she loved him. Often at night as he lay in bed, James would try to remember what his Mama had looked like. Having died when he was so small, James had no real memories of her. Over the years, though, he had begun to form an image of his Mama in his mind. That image was in every regard identical to his treasured sister Antoinette. If Mama was like anyone, she would have been like Antoinette, James assured himself.

"Marguerite, leave Antoinette alone!" scolded Daniel.

Daniel was two years younger than Marguerite, and of all his siblings, he was the most difficult for James to relate to. At times he was quite severe with James, seeming to enjoy making James' life more difficult than was necessary.

Daniel was strong, and an excellent hunter, often providing meat for the family, supplementing their meager diets. A blessing that all of them appreciated. James supposed that Daniel's natural toughness explained why he could be so severe. But then, without explanation, Daniel could at other times be such a sincere friend, going far beyond what any of his other siblings would ever consider doing, in order to procure some comfort for James. Perhaps these actions of kindness were driven by a sense of guilt for how he treated James. James had no idea.

There were only two things that James was absolutely sure of when it came to Daniel. Firstly, like himself, Daniel adored his sister Antoinette. James supposed that the death of Mama must have been much harder on Daniel than it was on him. Daniel had only been five years old. He imagined how much Antoinette must have coddled her little brother as she dried his tears. If anyone spoke harshly toward Antoinette, it was as certain as thunder following lightening that Daniel would soon be heard coming to her defense. This fact alone rose Daniel a few notches in James' eyes.

The second thing that James was certain of was that Daniel was loyal to family when it mattered most. Sure, Daniel might tease James when the two of them were alone, but James knew that his older brother would never allow anyone else to treat him poorly. Should some poor stranger attempt even the slightest insult toward James, he knew without hesitation that Daniel would be there to protect him, and perhaps even deal out a little punishment to the offending party.

James had learned early which of his two older brothers to take certain types of problems to. If he wanted counsel, he went to Jean. If he needed strength or revenge on some unsuspecting villager, he went to Daniel. To do the opposite would have been pointless. Jean would never have harmed a fly on James' behalf. Instead, he would have urged James toward forgiveness and patience. And Daniel was worth about as much as a brown bear when it came to asking for advice on important matters.

With summer now in full swing, the family worked hard to put away the food and supplies that they would need to survive the next long winter. A cycle that had repeated itself every year of James' young life. Long, boring winters followed by a very busy summer of work and toil, with only the Sabbath to rest. As the season wore on, the events of the three strange American preachers visiting their little temple faded into memory and were soon mostly forgotten by James, who had more important things to worry about.

August 1850

Chapter Three

A New Spring in the Valleys

"Daniel, LEAVE US ALONE!"

James and a neighbor boy by the name of Henri were sitting together, leaning against the rock wall that led to the family home. Henri's parents had tried for many years to have a son. And while the family had been blessed with several daughters, it wasn't until the sixth child that the Lord had seen fit to give them the boy they had wanted. So pleased had they been at his birth that they decided to name him after the great Henri Arnaud. Being named after a hero gave Henri something to live up to, but being named after the greatest hero of them all, the leader of the

Glorious Return, the most important champion of the Waldensian faith in the past 500 years, it was quite an honor for James' friend.

Henri was shorter than James, and about six months younger. The two had met the prior season during their first year of subsidiary. They had sat by each other, sharing a desk in the cold schoolhouse. Their daily proximity resulted in a friendship blossoming between them.

James didn't want to think about subsidiary right now. August had arrived in the tops of the mountains, and he and Henri would not have to return to their studies for nearly two months.

High above the rest of the world, the temperature remained relatively comfortable, even during what was the hottest part of summer everywhere else. It was one of the blessings that counterbalanced the difficult winters. Winters on the mountains were impossibly difficult. During that time of year few dared to venture outdoors. But summer was an altogether different season. Summer on the mountain tops was a season of warm light and blue skies. Never too hot, never too cool. Several consecutive months of what equated to spring weather everywhere else.

By now, the white snows of winter had finally all melted away, except for on the highest peaks. This melted snow thoroughly watering the mountainside, resulting in numerous wildflowers spontaneously springing to life. The mountain had adorned herself in her finest apparel. A deep forest of green peppered with purples, reds, yellows, pinks, and an assortment of many other impressive and dramatic shades of color that the adults seemed to admire.

Eleven year old James and his ten year old friend Henri were more inclined to pick these flowers and pulverize them into mushy balls than to bother appreciating them. For these young boys, the colors that dripped out of the tender petals were best applied to coloring rocks and fingers, not for smelling or enjoying in some other dull way.

What good does smelling them do? James and Henri had been working hard all morning, faithfully rubbing the petals from different flowers onto the rocks that lined their dirt lane. Each was deeply engrossed in this project. Streaks of faint red, yellow, and purple, mixed with bits of what had been flower parts ran down the handful of rocks that were closest to them.

As they rubbed the defenseless flowers along the rocks, James' and Henri's conversation meandered through a variety of topics, from how much they hated beets, to which of their neighbor's dogs would win in a fight. Now they were discussing whom among all of the ten year old girls in the area was the prettiest.

James was just starting to notice these young ladies, and as a result, he was now beginning to act differently around them. Somehow these girls, who had been his friends for as long as he could remember, now made him feel nervous and awkward. He didn't feel shy, though, when it came to talking about them. Indeed, doing so with his friend was an enjoyable way to pass the afternoon, however it was not a topic he wanted either of his brothers to overhear. Especially Daniel.

But it was too late for that. To James' dismay, Daniel had somehow managed to sneak up into the trees where he had perched, unnoticed by either James or Henri. A trick that he was proficient at. It was a skill that Daniel had spent years practicing so that he could be a better hunter. A tactic that James thought was all well and good for sneaking up on prey, but that Daniel should not be using against family.

James had been telling Henri that, in his opinion, no one was prettier than Catherine Beus, when Daniel unexpectedly leaped to the ground from a branch above them.

"Do you want me to go and get Catherine for you, James?" taunted Daniel. "I will tell her that you want to kiss her." He snidely prodded.

The embarrassment of being overheard by Daniel, along with the unexpectedness of his brother's sudden appearance had been what had caused James to shout, "Daniel, LEAVE US ALONE!"

"Oh, I will leave you alone alright. You and Catherine that is. You two are going to need all the privacy you can get so you can plan your wedding."

Daniel was fifteen years old. More than four years older than James, and several pounds heavier. James was scrawny and possessed nothing of manhood's frame or strength. Daniel, on the other hand, had grown strong early. When he had been James' age, Daniel had been both taller and also much stronger than James now was. That was four years ago. Since then, Daniel had grown larger and stronger than most of the full-grown men.

If James had been wise he would have taken this into account before he stood up and began to run directly toward his older brother. "Be quiet, you dumb ox!"

Daniel caught James by the head and easily swung him

about so that he could hold him with his arm around James' neck, Daniel then coolly replied, "A dumb ox, am I? That is not a very nice thing to say to your older brother."

"What do you say, Henri, do you think that we ought to show James how he should talk to his elders?"

Henri sat frozen in Daniel's gaze, not moving, as though he were trying to blend into the sturdy silence of the rocks behind him. Henri was smaller than James. If Daniel could so easily overpower James, then Henri did not stand a chance.

"What is the matter with your friend, James? Does he know how to speak, or is he even dumber than you?"

"I think we will teach you both a lesson. Take off your shoes." Daniel looked at the two terrified boys and repeated his order, but this time more forcefully. "I said, TAKE OFF YOUR SHOES!"

Daniel dropped James on the ground next to his friend. The two boys nervously obeyed, removing the old worn leather shoes that their families had fashioned for them.

Materials were scarce in the valleys. A boy was expected to take good care of his clothing. It took many hours and precious resources to make them. Losing or damaging these items would often mean going without. Families could not afford to fashion replacements. If a young man could not take care of the items he had been given, then as far as the adults were concerned, the boy did not deserve to have them. If you don't care for things like shoes, then you won't be trusted with a new pair.

James felt terrible. He should not have allowed his temper to get the better of him. Now not only would he suffer for getting angry, but so would his friend.

The Waldensian people walked everywhere they went. The mountain trails were littered with rocks, thorny plants, and other unfriendly obstacles. But of course, thought James, Daniel does not care about these things. Daniel would have fun watching them as their feet grew sore.

It wasn't fair. If James had been older, he would have been a kind brother. He would be someone that a younger brother could count on and look up to, unlike Daniel, who enjoyed making his life as difficult as possible.

As he considered this, an idea began to take root in James' mind, that offered him a bit of comfort. Papa was a fair man. James thought that if his Papa knew that it had been Daniel who had taken his shoes, then he would make Daniel give him HIS shoes. All he had to do was tell Papa what had happened, and then it would be Daniel who would go the rest of the season with bare feet, and not him.

As James and Henri sat barefoot along the rock wall, Daniel walked a short distance away. He carefully placed his stolen bounty on the ground in the space between the lane and the mountainside.

What was he doing? Could he have already tired of his game? Was he simply going to leave them there and wander off?

"I will be right back. If you move those shoes, you are dead!" Daniel warned.

They watched as Daniel walked off a short distance and then disappeared behind the nearby trees. After a few minutes, he returned. His arms were loaded down with old dead pine tree branches. Daniel placed these branches carefully around the boy's shoes. He left a second time, returning once again with his arms holding a large bundle of brown, dried out pine branches.

This continued several more times until there were old prickly branches surrounding the boys' shoes stretching out in every direction for several feet. Looking over his work, Daniel at last appeared to be satisfied. He then turned his glance to the younger boys, and with mocking concern said, "Now boys, you know you will be in trouble if you lose your shoes. So you better go and collect them!"

James' earlier hopes were immediately dashed. He would not be able to talk Papa into giving him Daniel's shoes after all. Nor would he easily be able to get his own back. James would have to walk across a bed of old sharp pine needles with nothing to protect the bottoms of his young soft feet. James determined that he would at least make sure that Henri would not share his humiliation. After all, there was no reason that they should both have to walk across Daniel's needle bed. One of them could collect both pairs of shoes.

As James gestured for Henri to remain seated, Daniel laughed, saying, "Oh no you don't. No cheating. James can't get your shoes for you. You either get them yourself, or you don't get them at all."

Crossing this menacing blanket of dead, twisted branches was slow and difficult. It took the boys several minutes. Within the first few steps their feet began to sting. By the time they were halfway across both of their feet had several little red marks where blood was beginning to appear. Occasionally one of their feet would slip off a branch, causing them to lose their balance. As they fell forward, their ankles and legs would get devoured by the unforgiving needles. The pain and injustice of their situation brought tears to James' eyes. He had to swallow hard to keep from crying. But he was brave. He did not let his brother see just how much he had hurt him. No doubt this is what Daniel wanted— to see him cry. James was not going to give him that victory.

James at last reached the center and carefully placed his shoes back onto his feet. James then looked back at Henri. He was several feet behind, on his hands and knees, crying. James glanced toward where Daniel had been enjoying their misery and realized that he was no longer there. He had left as quietly as he had come. Perhaps he was still nearby, watching from a branch, or from behind a boulder. James didn't care. He grabbed Henri's shoes and tossed them to him. James then helped Henri stand, and while supporting his balance watched Henri put his shoes back on. The two of them then ran off to find another, more safe place to spend the rest of their day.

Later that evening, as the sun was beginning to set behind the mountain, James returned home. It was still light outside, but it was getting darker. James climbed the old stone steps that led upstairs to the main room of their little cottage. It was here that the family spent most of their indoor time. The only room large enough to hold them all. The lower level was used as a sort of stable for the animals during the cold winter months.

Supper was not quite ready, so James took a seat in a dilapidated old wooden chair along one of the four small walls. After sitting down, he glanced over at his older brother Daniel. James did his best to look both tough and unbeaten. He wanted Daniel to know that he may be stronger but that his strength could not defeat him. Daniel could hold him down a thousand times, and each time James would get up again. One day, James hoped that he would be the one who was stronger, and Daniel the one who was weaker.

"And when I am stronger," he thought to himself "I will not attack Daniel unfairly. But on days like today, when he deserves it, I will teach him a lesson."

"Ah, boys, good, you are home." Papa entered the room through the same door that James had just used. His voice was warm and reassuring to James.

Papa was strong like Daniel, but that is where the

comparison between the two of them both began and ended. Papa was kind, loving, and thoughtful. He would do anything for James, and James knew it. He knew that no matter what happened, he could count on his Papa, who would be there to protect him. In this world he would never be alone. And that gave James tremendous comfort.

"What has everyone been up to today? How have you spent your Sabbath?"

Jean intimated that he had been reading a book which he had borrowed from a neighbor. Something that surprised no one, as Jean loved reading. Antoinette and Marguerite had both passed the time doing needlework; Marguerite for herself, and Antoinette for Papa.

"And what about you, Daniel? How have you spent your freedom?" Papa looked warmly toward Daniel.

"James and I played together in the lane, Papa," Daniel replied.

"Oh? What did you do?" sighed Papa as he sat down wearily.

"Not much, Papa. We were just seeing who had the most

endurance."

"That's great, boys." Papa leaned back against the wall, briefly closing his tired eyes as he rested his head against one of the cold round stones cemented into the wall.

James looked at Daniel disgustedly. He was furious. They had not been playing together as he had claimed. If Daniel had told Papa the truth, he would have said that he had been abusing James in the lane today.

Daniel looked into James' eyes. James was still upset and returned Daniel's glance with a venomous expression of disgust. As the two boys looked at each other, James saw what appeared to be regret briefly run across Daniel's face. Regret? Was that really what he had seen? Had Daniel been sorry for what he had done to him today?

If he was sorry, then why did he do it in the first place? What was the point of hurting someone, and then feeling sorry about it later? Or had Daniel not meant to hurt him? Had he meant what he said to Papa– that the two of them had been "playing" together? Had Daniel really believed that they were just playing together?

No. James decided that this was not possible. No one

could be that dumb. Daniel knew what he was doing. He was being mean. That is who Daniel was. A bully. And so what if he felt a momentary bit of regret later on? What mattered was that he had committed the offense, not that he had felt sorry about it.

Papa opened his heavy eyes and spoke in a quiet but firm voice to the room at large. "Daniel, I will be heading down to the markets tomorrow morning to pick up some cheesecloth and a few other supplies. I will need you to accompany me. James and Jean will do your morning chores for you."

Papa's announcement left James utterly depressed. First Daniel had picked on him, and now how would he be punished? He would get to skip his morning chores and would instead spend the time walking and talking with Papa!

James would be left behind.

James did not sleep well at all that night, which was unfortunate. He needed the strength that a good night's rest would provide. He would, after all, be doing extra chores the next day.

Each time that his mind had almost given in, allowing him to fall into a blissful state of forgetfulness, James would once again remember the events that had occurred earlier in the day. As he relived these memories, he got more and more frustrated. He was exhausted, but it didn't matter. He laid awake tossing back and forth under his thin wool blanket.

Eventually, long after Papa had begun to snore, James also fell into a restless sleep. Then without warning, and far too quickly, morning arrived.

Papa's voice rung through the morning air, bouncing off the rock walls alongside the sunlight.

"Antoinette, will you please see what you can do about this?" Papa said, gesturing to a ragged and often repaired old shirt. "I caught it on something while I was working in the orchard."

"This shirt isn't much more than a bunch of repairs all held together by worn out thread," sighed Antoinette. "It isn't going to last much longer."

"You are a fantastic seamstress, my dear, just like your mother. I know you can manage it." Papa walked over to where she was sitting and lovingly placed his hand on her back. "If this blight keeps up, we won't have any crops to trade. I may be stuck with this old shirt for a very long time."

Papa smiled as he turned around to where Daniel was

intently focused on sharpening the blade of the knife that he used to skin and gut the animals he hunted.

"Son, it's time. We need to get an early start, I have a lot of work to get done after we get back."

"Papa," answered Daniel slowly, "I don't feel up to a long walk this morning. I would rather stay here and work. Can James go with you instead?"

James was dumbfounded, and uncertain of what he had heard. Had Daniel really just passed on the opportunity to avoid morning chores? And more importantly, a chance to take a long walk alone with Papa? James looked up at Daniel in surprise. His eyes were again met by those of his brother. Daniel's face looked almost apologetic, compassionate even.

Surviving in the mountains meant working long difficult hours. During the warm season there were enough chores to keep everyone busy from the moment they awoke in the morning, until they went to bed at night. The opportunity to enjoy a nice long walk was something that you did not pass up. But this was not just any walk. It would be with Papa. James would have him all to himself. Papa would hold his hand, and the two of them would talk. Not even Antoinette, who James knew loved him so deeply, would have given up such an opportunity for him.

It just didn't make any sense. But the incomprehensibility of it aside, James was not about to turn down the offer.

"Yes, Papa. Please! I will carry back my share of whatever we buy in the market!" James did not mean to sound so enthusiastic, but his desire to walk to the valley floor with Papa overcame his self-control and betrayed his desperation.

Papa smiled, "Well, my boy, you are eleven now. Nearly a man. Yes . . . I think you can manage it!"

"Wait for me! Don't leave. I will grab my shoes," called out James as he ran out of the room and down the stairs.

James quickly slipped his shoes onto his feet, and then followed Papa out of the small yard that surrounded their cottage walking toward the lane. The two of them then set out, side by side, down the lane in the direction of the trails that led to the valley floor.

It was a beautiful morning. The sky was a shade of deep blue, interrupted only by a handful of low hanging soft white clouds. As they walked, James could hear several birds chirping and singing in the distant branches overhead.

After walking for a few minutes they reached the first trail that they would take. James knew it well. He had followed this path many times during his first season of subsidiary.

Although Papa was old, he was still strong and sure-footed. The steep terrain did not slow him down, his long legs easily maneuvering their way down the difficult trail.

It was difficult for James to keep up with him. James did not want Papa to think that he was slow or weak. Papa had said that he was nearly a man. Something that filled James with a sense of pride. If Papa thought he was a man, then James was not going to let him down. James ran, leaped, and did whatever he had to, in order to make sure that he did not slow his Papa down.

"My goodness, son. You sure have a lot of energy today," smiled Papa.

This compliment made James feel as lofty as the mighty hawk that was soaring in the sky high above them. Nothing mattered more to James than Papa's approval.

After several minutes of walking, Papa suggested that the two of them sit down for a few moments and rest. Although James did not admit it, he was grateful for the respite. Keeping up with Papa was difficult, and James was breathing heavily.

Papa sat down on a boulder that was situated beneath a large pine tree, casting its shade directly onto their rocky resting place. James climbed up with a little help from Papa and sat down beside him. He leaned over and placed his head on Papa's arm.

"My boy, you see this rock we are sitting on?" asked Papa, as he ran his hand along a white vein that ran through the rock.

James nodded.

"I can remember playing on this same rock when I was your age. That tree behind us was just as tall then as it is today. What do you think of that?"

James wasn't sure how his Papa expected him to answer. What did he think of it? Well, for one thing, that tree must be really old! If it was already full grown when Papa was his age, then it must be ancient. The trees around James' home didn't grow much at all. Each year, they were nearly the same height as they had been the year before. But certainly during a period of time as long as his Papa's life, all the trees in these mountains would have grown significantly taller. But he didn't think that this was what Papa wanted to hear, so he just smiled and shrugged his shoulders.

"You know what I think of, son, when I see this rock? It has sat here for decades, probably for thousands of years, exactly the same. The same cracks, the same bumps, unmoving, and unchanging."

James liked it when Papa spoke this way, whether he was talking about the stars, or the various animals and their uses, or in this case their mountainside. Papa was very wise, and listening to him fascinated James.

"James, my boy, can you think of anything else that is firm and unmovable like this rock? Something that has stood for thousands of years on this mountainside, unchanged by time?

James looked around. There were several trees, but James knew that they had not been there for thousands of years. At least he didn't think that they had been there that long. And they certainly did not remain unchanged. They were always changing; sprouting new branches, shedding old ones.

The animals had not been here unchanged for thousands of years. True, the same types of animals lived on the mountainside as probably had for generations, but not the same individuals. Like people, they were born as infants, they grew old, and eventually they died.

As James scanned the mountain, he saw off in the distance another medium-sized boulder. He shyly pointed to it and replied,

"That rock?"

Papa laughed and placed his arm around James, drawing him closer to his side while rubbing James' arm with his hand. "Yes, I suppose you are correct," he continued, still smiling. "But there is something else James. I will give you a hint. You are carrying it with you."

Now James was really confused. If it was unchanged and unmovable, then how could he be carrying it with him? He looked down at his hands. They were empty. All he had with him were his ragged and overly worn clothes and his tattered leather shoes.

"You carry it within you James. Something that has endured in these mountains for thousands of years, protected by the shade of these tall trees, and for that matter, James, protected by the mountain itself."

It finally dawned on James what his Papa was referring to. "The gospel of Jesus Christ, Papa?"

"YES, my boy!" cried Papa with delight. "You belong to a noble people, James. Never forget this."

The rest of the trek down the mountain was spent with Papa and James teasing each other. Papa would swing his leg that was opposite James backward behind his other leg, causing the side of his foot to softly strike James on his bottom. When James looked around there would be no one behind him. When he looked at Papa, he would appear completely innocent, as though he was admiring a distant squirrel. Papa would then repeat the action, once again seeming to be innocent of any offense.

"Papa!" James laughed.

"What? I didn't do anything!" Papa feigned offense.

Again, Papa struck James softly with his foot from behind. This time, James caught him in the act. "I knew it was you, Papa!" he exclaimed. James then attempted the same thing, but his legs were too short, and Papa was too quick.

By late morning, the two of them reached the valley floor, and made their way toward the market where people traded goods. There were a few worn out old shops, but most of those doing business in the market simply laid their various goods on the ground or on old tables.

"Jacques, how are you?" Papa greeted a man who had a variety of goods that he and his family had produced. "Do you have any cheesecloth?" he asked.

"Not much, but for you, Jean, you are welcome to whatever I have."

"Thank you. How is your family?" Papa inquired.

"Bless the Lord, we are all well. My little nephew, Joseph Gay, had been ill. He is only three years old. For a time, we thought that we were going to lose him. But he is now fully recovered."

Losing little ones was not uncommon in the valleys. Mountain life was a difficult existence. The slightest illness could quickly become exaggerated. Things that were considered mild infirmities in other regions could devastate the health of an individual here. With virtually no medicine, few doctors, and poor nutrition, life, it seemed, was always balanced on a knife's edge.

"Bless the Lord," affirmed Papa. "What was it that he contracted? Is anyone else in your family sick?"

"It was the strangest thing. The lad was fine one day, and the next he could hardly draw breath. He had a terrible fever, Jean. Nothing that we did for him helped."

"What a frightening experience, but it sounds as though the Lord was looking over your family," stated Papa.

"Jacques, do you also have any twine? We are running low."

"No, I am sorry. But I believe that the Torres do."

As Papa paid Jacques for the cloth, he asked, "What finally made the difference with your nephew? What did your family do that helped him?"

"It wasn't us. As I said, we did everything we could think of, but nothing helped. It was the Mormons that healed him!"

"The Mormons?" Papa repeated, in a questioning tone.

"Three preachers from America. They laid their hands on little Joseph's head and prayed to God to make him well. It wasn't but a few days after this blessing that the little guy was back up on his feet, active as he ever had been," smiled Jacques. "If those Mormon preachers had not come around when they did, Jean, we would have lost little Joseph, I am certain of it!"

During the hike back to their farm, James thought about what he had overheard. James knew that Christ and his apostles had healed people, but he had never heard of anyone being healed in modern times. Although he supposed that if healing was possible back then, it must still be possible today. But if healing was possible, then why didn't the barbes heal people? With all the sickness that existed here in the valleys, why didn't they just heal everyone?

"Papa, why don't the barbes heal people?" James thoughtfully asked.

"James, my boy, that is a very intelligent question. What a smart young man you are to think about such things." Papa did not, however, answer the question. He instead simply let it hang in the air throughout the remainder of their hike home.

1850

Chapter Four

Wherever the Spirit May Lead You

"It is not the quantity, brothers, but the quality that matters." Lorenzo Snow spoke to no one in particular, as he and his two companions sat together, dining on a scant meal of dried fruit and rabbit meat.

They had arrived in the valleys seven months earlier. At first, the Waldensian people had seemed to be receptive to the outsiders. They had invited them to preach in their little church houses, and to meet with their preachers. Given the warmth with which they had initially been welcomed into the Alps, Lorenzo had

had great hopes for the work here.

The Waldensian preachers had been glad to receive them, until they realized that the Americans meant to baptize the people that they taught into the Mormon faith. These preachers had a long history of sharing the gospel with their neighbors. In particular, as Lorenzo Snow and his companions had since learned, with the Protestants who had gained strongholds in numerous European nations. But these Protestants hadn't ever attempted to change the Waldensian's faith. They had come, preached, and then left. And after they were gone, the barbes were once again the unquestioned religious leaders of the alpine heights.

If Lorenzo and his companions hadn't attempted to convert anyone, then they would have continued to be allowed to preach openly in the Waldensian temples. But Lorenzo knew that this was not possible. The Lord had not sent them across the world to simply teach. They were tasked with sifting through the people in order to gather in the Lord's elect. Those whom he had prepared to hear the gospel message.

This meant baptizing them, and then organizing these new converts into congregations. Congregations that would of a necessity need to meet separately from the rest of the inhabitants, and away from the authority of the barbes.

It was a foreign notion and completely unfathomable. No one met separately! There was no faith other than that which the barbes professed! It was blasphemous to even consider meeting outside of their authority.

Lorenzo thought to himself that perhaps he would have done things differently if he had realized this when they first arrived. Perhaps he would have been more careful in disclosing their intentions.

When they first came to the valleys they interpreted the tender and welcoming attitude of the people as a sign that they were ready to hear their message. They had thought that surely the people upon these mountains were ripe for the harvest, and so they had moved quickly. Perhaps too quickly.

With the eagerness of someone holding a great treasure, they had worked day and night in an effort to share it with as many people as would listen. And at first, many did. But when Lorenzo and his companions began to teach that the Waldensians should leave the traditions of their people behind, and join themselves to the Mormon Church the attitudes of the people towards them changed instantly.

The Americans had been banned for several weeks now from entering any of the people's churches. The barbes had labeled them as troublemakers and workers of darkness. As a result, every door that had once been open was now shut, and shut firmly!

Lorenzo didn't know how he could have acted differently. The message he carried was, after all, true. He was sent by the Lord to share it, and share it he would. He couldn't see how they could convert anyone without first disclosing that this was their goal. And in any event, attempting to do so would have been dishonest. The Lord expected his servants to behave in an honorable fashion. Still, thought Lorenzo, he wished there had been a way to hold on to the initial spirit that had first followed them here. If only they could have preached to more people, or if the barbes had not become so negative and had not worked against them, then perhaps they would have found more converts among this ancient Christian sect.

Of course their words had not all been carried away by the mountain winds. Some of them had landed, like seeds, on fertile ears. Jean Antoine Bose had entered the waters of baptism. And the family of a little boy whom they had healed were reading the Book of Mormon together, although for now that family was unwilling to leave the safety of their Waldensian congregation. And Lorenzo could hardly blame them. Everyone this family knew was Waldensian. Every friend, associate, and family member. Everyone that they had ever known, or for that matter, were ever likely to know. And what would they be leaving to? A single convert? Hardly a congregation. It would take a great deal of faith indeed for anyone to leave the strength of a community that surrounded them, and join a tiny congregation of "heretics" that were professing a "work of darkness," as their preachers described the Mormons.

Lorenzo's heart was heavy as he considered the missionary work in this region and what would now have to be done. It would be very difficult to leave the Alps behind, and especially their single convert. How would Brother Bose get along without them?

"Joseph, I feel impressed to send you on to Sicily, to the house of your people. You know the culture there, and you have many friends and family relations. Go and preach the gospel to your homeland."

Lorenzo looked over his tin cup at Joseph Toronto. He looked tired. Joseph had crossed the plains with his family, begun to build a farm, then crossed the plains again in the other direction.

He had then crossed the Atlantic Ocean on a ship, worked tireless hours in London, then traveled to the Alps. "There is little rest for the faithful," Lorenzo had begun to say, but was interrupted by Joseph.

Joseph's eyes lit up. "Brother Snow, I have been praying for this opportunity. Since finding the gospel, I have wanted nothing more than to bring it home to my family. Please do not worry. The Lord will look after me, and I will find converts among my family and friends there."

Joseph's faith and spirit had the effect of also lifting Lorenzo. He was impressed by his enthusiasm and zeal for the gospel.

"Thomas, I feel that the Lord wants you and I to travel to Switzerland. I believe that he has prepared souls in Geneva for the gospel message." Lorenzo now looked at Thomas Stenhouse.

Although he had not had to come as far from home as Lorenzo Snow and Joseph Toronto, he looked even more tired than the two of them combined. Stenhouse had not grown up on the frontier as had Snow, and he was not used to physical work as was Toronto. He had spent his entire life living in the heart of the most powerful empire on Earth, that of the British. Even though his family had not been terribly wealthy, they had always had sufficient for their needs. His had been a life of schooling and scholarly work. He had been wholly unprepared for the trials of missionary life.

Despite how tired he looked, Lorenzo Snow had to admit though that the man never complained. He worked just as hard as everyone else. He might have been a little slower, but it was not for a lack of effort. And now, several months later, he was nearly as strong and fast as the other two men.

"If Geneva is where the Lord wants us, Elder Snow, then to Geneva we will travel," Stenhouse answered without hesitation.

"What about the work here, Brother Lorenzo? What about Jean Bose, and the Gay family?"

Lorenzo Snow could feel the genuine concern and love in the words of Thomas Stenhouse's voice. "Joseph, you will leave immediately for Sicily. Thomas and I will remain behind a few more months before setting off for Geneva. I have written to a young convert in London. Thomas, I believe you know him. A Jabez Woodard."

"Brother Woodard? Yes, indeed I do. A very faithful saint if ever there was one," smiled Thomas.

"Yes, well, I have asked him to travel to these mountains and serve here as Mission President in my stead. He will continue the work with Jean Bose, and will teach the Gay family. And with the Lord's blessing, perhaps he will find many additional converts among the Waldensians," Lorenzo concluded.

A few days later, Joseph Toronto bid farewell to his brothers in the gospel, and faithfully set out for his homeland. Joseph would have to travel across the entire length of Italy on foot to reach Sicily, but he was excited to do so, hardly able to contain his impatience to share the pearl of great price that he had discovered in America.

A month later, the young Jabez Woodard arrived from London and was greeted warmly by Lorenzo Snow and Thomas Stenhouse. Jabez looked as fresh and soft as Thomas Stenhouse once had. Like Thomas, Jabez had also spent his entire life in the midst of civilization, comfort, learning, and bookwork. But this was who the Lord had inspired Snow to call as Mission President in the valleys, and for Lorenzo that was sufficient.

Jabez Woodard's extra half-inch of fat, his soft hands, untanned skin, and complete naivete at the experience he was about to have did not disqualify him in the least. It was his spirituality, his humility, and his ability to faithfully lead in the gospel that mattered to the Lord. And in this regard, Jabez was more than an adequate fit for the task that the Lord was giving him.

Jabez had a strong and firm testimony of the restoration of the gospel, and he was not afraid to share it. He was a little shy at times, but not so much so that he let it hold him back. When it was time to testify, he did so. When it was time to preach, he was always able to find his tongue, and once he began to speak, Lorenzo knew that the Lord would take care of the rest, giving him the words that he should say.

After spending several weeks with Jabez, showing him the valleys, introducing him to Brother Bose and to the Gay family, and instructing him in his mission, Lorenzo Snow and Thomas Stenhouse were at last ready to move on to Geneva, Switzerland.

"Brother Woodard, Thomas and I will head north tomorrow. Before we leave, I would like to spend some time with you in the mountain peaks"

Lorenzo pointed over their tent and upward to a spire that reached beyond the heights of the nearby clouds.

"We have no dedicated temple to worship the Lord in

Brothers, but we will find that his Spirit rests more abundantly upon those mountain peaks."

It took the three men most of the morning to hike up the nearest peak. Alone at the summit, they knelt together in prayer. Each man took a turn praying aloud. They petitioned the Lord for their families back home, their wives and children, who were alone. They prayed for Brother Toronto, who was somewhere in Italy, wandering toward Sicily. They prayed for the work in Switzerland. They then prayed fervently over the land that lay before them. The land of the Waldensians. Lorenzo Snow dedicated the region for missionary work once again, reaffirming their commitment to the task of finding the elect who lived there. In his prayer, Lorenzo Snow named the peak that they stood on as, "The Rock of Prophecy." He also named another nearby peak as, "Mount Brigham," after the Lord's living prophet.

After the three men finished praying, Lorenzo Snow laid his hands upon the head of Jabez Woodard. He ordained the young father to the office of High Priest, and set him apart as the Mission President over the missionary work in the Waldensian valleys.

Lorenzo Snow then laid his hands upon the head of

Thomas Stenhouse, and also ordained him to the office of High Priest in the Melchizedek Priesthood. Afterward, the three men descended the mountain feeling revitalized, having their spirits refreshed and renewed.

"Thomas, before we set out for Geneva, I need to write a letter to my quorum leader. He is expecting a report from me."

Lorenzo Snow secluded himself in his tent and took a few hours to pen a letter to Orson Hyde, the President of the Quorum of the Twelve Apostles. Lorenzo updated him on the progress of the missionary work in Europe. In his letter, he expressed his love for the people of the alpine valleys, and his sadness at moving on to Geneva before seeing more of them enter into the waters of baptism.

". . . there is a poem that was written about the people of these valleys which I would like to include in my letter to you, President Hyde. It describes perfectly their romantic situation, protected as they are by their mountain fortress. This poem is entitled 'The Mountain Christians.'

For the strength of the hills we bless thee,

Our God, our fathers' God;

Thou hast made thy children mighty,

By the touch of the mountain sod.

Thou hast fixed our ark of refuge

Where the spoiler's foot ne'er trod.

For the strength of the hills we bless thee,

Our God, our fathers' God.

We are watchers of a beacon

Whose light must never die;

We are guardians of an altar

'Midst the silence of the sky.

The rocks yield founts of courage,

Struck forth as by Thy rod;

For the strength of the hills we bless thee,

Our God, our fathers' God.

For the dark resounding caverns,

Where Thy still, small voice is heard;

For the strong pines of the forests,

That by Thy breath are stirred;

For the storm, on whose free pinions,

Thy spirit walks abroad;

For the strength of the hills we bless thee,

  Our God, our fathers' God.

The royal eagle darteth

  O'er his quarry from the heights,

And the stag, that knows no master,

  Seeks there his wild delights;

But we, for Thy communion,

  Have sought the mountain sod.

For the strength of the hills we bless thee,

  Our God, our fathers' God.

The banner of the chieftain,

  Far, far below us waves;

The war-horses of the spearman

  Cannot reach our lofty caves.

Thy dark clouds wrapt the threshold

  Of freedom's last abode.

For the strength of the hills we bless thee,

  Our God, our fathers' God.

For the shadow of Thy presence

Round our camp of rock outspread;

For the stern defiles of battle,

Bearing record of our dead;

For the snows and for the torrents,

For the free heart's burial sod;

For the strength of the hills we bless thee,

Our God, our fathers' God.

"This poem was written by a Misses Felcia Hemans from London, who had been inspired by her travels among this noble people. I will write you again, President Hyde, after I arrive in Switzerland."

July 1851 – December 1852

Chapter Five

The Light of the World

The faithful fig trees that grew around Mama's grave were
among the few crops that had not been utterly devastated by the
blight. These and other trees, such as those that bore chestnuts or
mulberries.

Mama had loved figs. When she died, Papa had planted
several of them around her grave on the family farm. Each year
since, these trees had faithfully yielded a bountiful crop, as though
Mama were wielding influence from heaven, making sure that her
little family didn't starve.

The rye, wheat, and oats had all been sparse this year. The

vegetable garden looked as though it too would not produce a sufficient crop for James and his family. The blight that had begun in the lower portions of the mountains a few years earlier had now spread throughout the entire region, like a tenacious fog, casting a shadow of starvation wherever it fell.

All over the mountain people were hungry, tired, and concerned about the coming winter. If they couldn't get their crops to grow, then they wouldn't eat, and without food, they would die. There were already reports of some who had succumbed to this horrible fate, though James had no idea if these stories were true.

What he did know was that when they walked down to the markets, there were many very hungry looking children, begging for the smallest morsel of food. These children were desperate for any scrap or crumb that they could get their scrawny hands on. They were not aggressive or pushy. They simply sat alongside the various dirt roads and held out their hands toward passersby. To James, they looked like they might be asking for someone to hold them, as much as to feed them. Papa explained that many of these children had homes and families just like James, but these homes had no food. In desperation, their parents had sent them out to fend for themselves. At least in so far as eating was concerned.

They returned each night to sleep in their homes and to be with their parents. But if they wanted to eat, they had to leave each morning and beg, or forage on the mountainside.

James' family was hungry, too, but Papa had so far always managed to find enough to feed them all each day. Not as much as in happier times, but enough to keep them alive.

Daniel had been critical to this effort. He was a skilled hunter. Papa bragged that Daniel was even better than he himself had been. Most days he would bring home a rabbit, a squirrel, or a few birds. Occasionally he was able to find and kill larger prey, such as deer or chamois. These were especially wonderful treats. On such occasions, no one in the family went to bed hungry. As Marguerite prepared the meal, everyone would laugh and enjoy the company of one another. The savory smell of roasting meat hanging thick in the air. On those days, no one went to bed hungry.

By supplementing the family's scant supplies with wild meat, and through Papa's careful efforts in storing grains and preserving fruits, nuts, and other edible items, the family had managed to remain self-sufficient. But their supplies were getting low. If this blight continued on much longer, they would be just as destitute as were many of the other mountain inhabitants.

The barbes were particularly worried. They had done everything in their power to help the needy. Splitting up and walking along the mountainside, they visited each and every home, some more than once. They inquired of the needs that each family had that were not being met, and into any excess that a family might have and if they might be willing to share some of that excess with others.

Unfortunately, the needs far outweighed the excesses. Everywhere they went families had long lists of needs: Food, clothing, ailing physical health, problems with livestock, and a host of other things that they complained about to the barbes. And virtually nowhere was there anyone who had an item that they didn't need, and would be able to part with.

This dire situation did not, however, dampen the faith of the people. Nor did it keep the barbes from attending to their duties on the Sabbath. On Sunday, the people came together in prayer and worship. Sure times were difficult, but these difficulties would not endure forever. Their faith in their God, on the other hand, that was indeed eternal.

As they entered the temple for Sunday services in late

autumn, Papa, Jean, Daniel, and James sat down on the right side of the room, while Antoinette and Marguerite took their seats opposite them on the left. The atmosphere in the chapel was friendly enough, albeit solemn. People were burdened but not beaten. They were concerned about the difficulties that they all faced, but determined to overcome them.

As the congregation sat in reverence, Barba Peyrot took the podium.

"My dear, blessed friends. My beloved people. It pains me to see so much suffering among you. But let us draw comfort from the scriptures!" Barba Peyrot pointed to heaven and proclaimed, "Remember what Christ said about hunger! 'Let those who hunger follow after me, and I shall feed them.'"

"Now, I know, my dear friends, that the word of God does not fill your stomachs, but with empty stomachs and humble hearts, we are sometimes more able to feast upon the word of God. And by feasting upon the word of God, our souls will be filled. My dear friends, what is a momentary bit of physical hunger compared to an eternity of spiritual hunger?"

Barba Peyrot spoke for several more minutes on the virtues of partaking of the word of God so as to feed one's soul. Near the end of his sermon, he changed topics.

"Now, my dear friends, I wish to warn you of a great evil that has come into our valleys. A wicked pack of wolves who wear sheep's clothing, and who go about proclaiming that they represent the Lord. I am here to tell you the truth about these unrighteous preachers of sin so that you will not be led astray by their lies!"

Barba Peyrot's tone of voice was rising. It was now much louder than it had been during the first part of his sermon. Several of the men who had silently drifted to sleep were now wide awake, listening intently.

With fire in his eyes, Barba Peyrot continued, "What do these devils call themselves? Mormons! They go about preaching of pretended and false prophets, and of forged scriptures. Works of darkness, RUBBISH!" he shouted.

"They bind men down with lies. Oh yes, my friends. Wicked and deceitful lies, designed to fool the children of God's mountain into betraying their heritage.

"These wicked men have come from America. And who sent them? T'was Satan himself! For Satan has tried many times to destroy God's work upon these sacred mountains. He sent armies to attack us. And were they successful? NO! Because our mountains protected us! But now, I am afraid, my dear friends, yes indeed, I am afraid, lest Satan should finally gain his prize! This time Satan has sent something far more dangerous than armies! False prophets to destroy with misguided words!

"If you should encounter these vile creatures, you must close your doors to them. Do not engage them in conversation. They are sly and will use any opportunity to confuse you– to lead you astray! And from there, down to Hell itself!"

"Now, my friends, go forth in faith and prayer until we meet again next Sunday!"

James was frightened by Barba Peyrot's words. He wondered what the servants of hell would look like? Surely they must look terrifying. As he tried to imagine them with horns, James suddenly remembered what Jacques had told Papa several months earlier about his little nephew, Joseph Gay, who had been healed by the Mormons. Were these the same Mormons that Barba Peyrot had spoken of? Surely they must be. How many Mormons could there be?

But why would the Gay family allow such wicked men into their home? James wondered if Papa would have allowed servants of the devil to heal him if he were dying.

"Papa," James looked up to the massive frame of his dear Papa, darkened as it was by the sun, which shone above him in the sky. The sky was a soft blue, blended into light gray, a sign that winter was not far off. The walk home from temple was cool enough to make James uncomfortable. Conversation would help take his mind off of the temperature of his skin.

James felt safe asking his Papa about the Mormons. Other adults might not understand his question, but Papa always listened, and never scolded him for asking questions. "Were the . . . the Mormons that Barba Peyrot warned us about . . . were they the same . . . Mormons that healed Joseph Gay?"

"Yes, my boy, I believe that they were the very same."

"Papa, why would they allow them into their home? Why would they let those men near their son?"

"James, do you remember when the Mormons preached in our temple?"

James had not thought about the sermon Papa was mentioning since that Sunday more than a year earlier. He was lucky if a sermon stayed with him longer than ten minutes once he left the temple. His mind was usually too full of thoughts of how he would spend his free afternoons to worry about what the old barbes had been saying. But in this case, he did remember. It had been a strange enough experience to stand out in his memory.

"Yes, Papa, I do remember them." James thought for a moment then continued, "Papa . . . they did not seem wicked."

"No, my boy, they did not," smiled Papa.

Papa did not offer any more counsel, and James did not inquire further. Instead, he walked in silence, considering the events of the day. On the one hand, the Mormons seemed to be very nice people. Misguided and full of odd ideas, true. But honorable men. On the other hand, Barba Peyrot had preached against them, saying that they were servants of the devil himself. But if they were really servants of the devil, thought James, then why had the barbes allowed them into temple in the first place? If they were evil, wouldn't the barbes have spotted them immediately, and turned them away?

Autumn brought little relief from the blight. Although there was sufficient water to wet the ground, and although the people worked many long hours in their fields, the mountain still refused to relinquish her crops. In the place of a bounteous harvest, there was instead an ever growing crisis, increasing daily in scope and severity. Everyone, even the most well-prepared, were hungry.

Any bit of storage or reserves were all but gone.

The only crops that were not affected were the trees that bore their various fruits and nuts. The blight only seemed to affect those crops that grew on the ground. There had been a bounteous harvest of mulberries, figs, and now that fall was here, the chestnuts were at last coming on.

Many times over the centuries these chestnuts had been the salvation of James' people. They grew naturally across the mountains, requiring no real effort on the part of the people. Each tree provided a large crop, and there were many trees. Soon they would be everywhere. Food would literally be raining down from heaven onto the forest floor. And when this occurred, the hungry would at last have something with which to fill their stomachs. It wasn't enough to sustain them for an entire year, but it would be enough to get the people through the next few months.

During which, they could gain a little weight and lose a little despair. Which was good, because winter would follow closely behind autumn, and when it did, the people would then face the grim and brutal reality of life on the mountains. With their food stores barren, and with the high snows preventing most from leaving their homes, winter was going to try the spirit of this people in a way that had not happened for several generations.

Before winter took over the mountainside completely, and while it was still possible to make the trek to temple, James was once again tasked with making a daily trek to subsidiary.

Now in his third year, he was no longer one of the youngest students, and that was a great feeling. His first year, James had been petrified by the prospect of attending subsidiary. He hadn't known what to expect. After spending the first ten years of his life largely on the family farm, and almost entirely in the company of the same five companions, he would, for the first time in his life, be spending several hours a day away from his family, and with people he either had never met, or at least had not frequently been around.

He had known many of the boys from their games on the mountains. And he also had known Barba Peyrot since virtually the day he had been born. But knowing them, and spending almost all your time with them for four months, were two very different things.

This year was different. This year James was looking forward to returning. Subsidiary was no longer a mysterious and foreboding place. The people there were no longer mere passing acquaintances. They were his friends. Friends who, after spending many hours together during the previous two seasons, he now knew very well.

James had probably left earlier than he needed to on his first morning, but he couldn't sleep, and he didn't want to be late. As he hiked towards the little temple where subsidiary was held, his heart felt light and free. Even under the burden of a heavy load of chestnuts, James felt as though he could almost glide down the mountain like a great eagle. He settled instead for leaping from boulder top to boulder top.

When James arrived outside the temple door he was alone. The door to the temple did not lock, but James knew better than to enter. It would have been disrespectful. One of the barbes might be spending the night inside. They could be sleeping, or praying, or preparing a sermon.

James contented himself to instead find a comfortable place outside. He carefully laid down in the grasses that surround the little building and rested his head on the stone foundation. As he impatiently awaited the arrival of some of the other boys, James repeatedly threw a small stone into the air above his hands so that it would fall straight down. Catching it, he would then repeat the action by tossing it up again.

After several minutes a few of the other boys began to arrive. As these boys waited for one of the barbes to open the temple door, they chatted about their families and the experiences that they had had since last seeing each other.

"Henri!" James shouted across the little field that separated the temple from the forest. Henri looked up and smiled at James. His parted lips revealing a few missing teeth. "Hey, Henri! I lost some of my teeth, too. Look!"

The two friends laughed and then walked a short distance from the others where they sat down together, and began to eagerly discuss what the day might bring.

After a few more minutes Henri blurted out something that he had clearly been anxious to say to James.

"I bet I can beat you in an arm wrestle!" Henri challenged.

James was bigger and stronger than Henri. He had no idea what would make Henri believe that he could beat him, but he wasn't about to allow him to remain in his confused state.

"I can beat you with a single finger," replied James. "I can beat you with my small finger, even if you used both arms," he teased.

"Well, then," prodded Henri. "If you are so sure, then let's do it."

The two boys laid down on the ground facing each other. They grasped hands and looked each other squarely in the eyes.

"One, two, THREE!" counted James.

The contest was over almost before it started and to James' shock, he was on the losing end.

Henri laughed, "My Papa taught me a trick. It is not how strong you are, but how you hold the other person's hand. Here, I will show you."

Henri showed James that if he grasped his opponent by the thumb and twisted it back, the opponents wrist would follow their thumb, and then their arm would follow their wrist.

"The wrist is weak. If you try to beat their arm, you will lose, but if you take on their wrist, you will win every time!" Henri was delighted that his trick had worked. He had obviously been practicing.

As the two sat in the wild grasses perfecting their new advantage and planning how they would use it against some of the other boys, Barba Peyrot opened the temple door. "Good morning, boys!" he smiled widely. "I am so glad to see you back here this season, and all safely."

The barbes took turns instructing the young men. The boys never knew who their teacher would be. Sometimes the same barba would instruct them for a week or more, other times they would get a new teacher every single day. It all depended on the business that the barbes had to attend to. But of all the barbes that passed through subsidiary, Barba Peyrot was the most common. He instructed them frequently because he was responsible for their temple; it was where he preached on Sundays.

Some of the barbes traveled extensively across the three Waldensian valleys. These perfects traveled because they were not assigned to a congregation. Others had responsibilities that kept their labors to a more defined region. The latter was the case for Barba Peyrot. But his calling did often require him to be away during the hours that subsidiary was held; duties such as visiting a family, sitting with a widow, or performing a marriage. And so, while he was frequently involved in the boys' education, he was not, by any means, the only barba that they encountered.

James thought that Barba Peyrot was an excellent teacher. He was not boring or dull, as some of the barbes were. And he was not mean or intimidating. He liked the children, and as a result, the children liked him. That was not to say that he was a pushover. The boys respected him. They knew that he would not put up with any guff or allow them to get away with misbehavior. There was a high expectation from him that each of the boys tried to live up to. He just seemed to connect with the boys, and they with him. James didn't care so much whether or not the other barbes thought he was a good boy, but he couldn't imagine disappointing Barba Peyrot. And this motivation made James work hard in his studies.

Their day was split between learning how to read and memorizing scriptures. Reading was considered to be important because it facilitated their study of the Bible. Learning the Bible was the real focus of subsidiary. It was why they were there— to prepare them for a lifelong love of the scriptures so that they could fulfill the mission that their people had been entrusted with by the Lord. Everyone learned to read; the boys at subsidiary, and the girls at home. And everyone memorized the scriptures.

Half of the benches that filled the chapel on Sunday had been pushed to one side of the room. In their place, a number of long wooden tables had been placed between the now more thinly dispersed benches that remained. The boys took their seats, and Barba Peyrot began by opening subsidiary with a prayer that he had prepared. After reading the prayer, Barba Peyrot looked around the room, making eye contact with each boy.

"My, my, such fine looking men! So strong and intelligent! So respectful and reverent! So ready to learn!" He smiled. "Let's see if you have been practicing, shall we? Or did you forget everything we learned last season?

"Arnauld, you are a year four, correct?"

"Yes, Barba," Arnauld replied.

"Tell us then, Arnauld, what are the be-attitudes?"

Without hesitation, Arnauld repeated several verses of scripture by heart from the New Testament. James was both impressed and also terrified. If Barba Peyrot had asked him about the be-attitudes he would not have known more than a couple of them, and he certainly would not have been able to repeat them from memory. In their first season they had spent most of their time focused on trying to learn how to read. Last season they had only memorized the ten commandments, and a few other passages of scripture that related to the story of Moses.

"Excellent, Arnauld! Excellent. You have made many generations of your forefathers proud with that wonderful recitation of scripture."

"Now, let's pick on a third year student." Those in the room who were attending for their third season sat up straighter and seemed to become a little uncomfortable.

"Jaon, what did the Lord deliver to Moses upon the Mount of Sinai?"

Jaon was not as fast in his reply as Arnauld had been. He looked cautiously up at his instructor before answering. "The, err, Ten Commandments, Barba," Jaon said, a bit unsure of himself.

"Very good, son. And what are the Ten Commandments?"

Jaon did his best to recite them. It took several uncomfortable minutes and a few false starts, but with occasional prompting by Barba Peyrot, he got through it successfully.

James admired the way Barba Peyrot had helped Jaon. He had not embarrassed him, but he had also not let him off the hook. If Barba Peyrot had allowed Jaon to give up, then Jaon would have felt like a failure. Many of the barbes would have grown impatient and moved on to someone else. But Barba Peyrot understood the importance of success and achievement. He allowed Jaon, with a bit of assistance, to succeed. James looked over at the boy, who was half a year older than himself; he sat proudly and tall upon his bench.

"Now, shall we pick on another third year student?" James dreaded what he was sure was coming. Barba Peyrot was a close family friend. He had visited their family farm often over the years. James was sure that he would call on him to recite some passage of scripture. James searched his mind trying to come up with something else that he had memorized. But as he explored the many crevices of his brain, he found it almost completely empty. Was he supposed to have memorized something else this year besides the ten commandments, in between seasons of subsidiary? Had he been assigned to work on passages and then in his eagerness to play forgotten to do it?

"James?"

"Yes, Barba?" James spoke over butterflies that he was certain everyone in the room could hear fluttering in his chest.

Barba Peyrot smiled and looked at James directly in the eyes, "James, can you please share for us the Waldensian motto?"

Relief washed over James. This was an easy question. Papa

had made him memorize their motto almost as soon as he could talk. "In darkness, light," James answered proudly.

"Correct!" replied Barba Peyrot, smiling broadly. "Very good, child. Very good indeed!

"Now, my dear first and second year boys, you see these fine examples before you? I could have called on anyone of them, and they would have answered my questions equally well. And that is what I will expect of you." Barba Peyrot looked at each of the younger boys. "Look to these older boys, study as hard as they do, and next year, when it is your turn to answer my questions, you will do as well as they did today, I know you will!"

The exercise had been very effective. Every boy in the class sat tall. Everyone of them not only understood what was expected of him, but they each also believed that they could accomplish it. Now they were ready to begin another season of hard scholarly work and study so that they would not disappoint Barba Peyrot, their families, or the Lord.

James in particular committed himself to his studies. He would work harder than he had the prior two seasons. He would take his lessons home with him and review them each evening.

And this he did. As the season drew to a close, James had

successfully memorized the be-attitudes forward and backward. He had also memorized a handful of other scriptures from the accounts of Luke, and the other four gospels. James imagined what it must have been like to live in ancient times, and to have heard apostles speak, and to observe with your own eyes the miracles that Christ had performed.

While James kept himself busy with his studies, winter inevitably chased autumn out of the valleys. In time the snows grew too deep to once again allow anyone to do much of anything outside. These heavy snows meant that this Sunday would be their family's last trip of the year to temple. After that, they would settle in for a long winter alone, cut off from the rest of their people.

The hike to temple was cold and unpleasant. It took far more effort to make the journey now that the snows were, in many places, as high as James' knees. To make the trek somewhat more manageable, he tried to step as often as possible in Papa's tracks. But Papa's legs were much longer than James', making it impossible for him to reach his widely spaced footprints more than every other step or so.

By the time they reached temple, James was both hot and sweaty, while at the same time also very cold. The effort of the trip had made parts of his body warm. However, his feet, hands and ears were experiencing the opposite extreme. They were purple and frozen. Worse of all, his pant legs were soaked, making him miserable and insuring that he would not be able to warm up, as he sat on the bench inside of the cold chapel. There was a fire burning, but it did not add much heat to the room, except for those lucky enough to be sitting near it.

Each member of the family kept their discomfort to themselves. Papa had taught them well, being clear in their duties. There was no point in complaining, when you already knew the answer that Papa would reply with.

"We do not miss temple unless we absolutely have to. Not unless one of us is deathly ill. As long as the snows are not too deep, we will make the trip."

And they did make the trip. Week after week. Long after many other families had stopped coming. They would have continued to attend temple next week too, and the week after that, but Barba Peyrot had informed them during the prior week's sermon that this would be the last service of the year. The barbes did not want to put anyone's lives at risk. As winter took hold upon the mountain tops, it was not practical for anyone to leave their homes. Not even for the purpose of worshiping the Lord. Their worship could take place much more safely at home. The Lord understood.

"My dear and faithful friends, so many of you still making the long, difficult walk to temple. Like the Lord's faithful sheep, coming to drink at the well of truth and righteousness." Barba Peyrot began his sermon in a warm tone that made his love for the people evidently clear.

Today's sermon was short. In cooler times they usually were. It was difficult for the people to sit very long when they were all suffering from a lack of warmth.

"And now, my friends, as winter once again forces us to go our separate ways for a season, I wish to leave upon you all a prayer of blessing from the Lord."

Barba Peyrot then began to read a prayer that he had prepared. This prayer called upon the Lord to look after the faithful members of the congregation as they secluded themselves in their various homes. That they might all emerge again the following spring, healthy, happy, and ready to face a new and better season. He asked the Lord to bless their mountains that the blight would disperse and that the people would again be able to grow their crops and provide for their families. His prayer continued in a similar manner, seeking blessings upon various individuals, widows, orphans, and upon those with a variety of ailments.

At the conclusion of his prayer, he continued his sermon with a renewed caution on a familiar topic. Barba Peyrot had warned his people about the dangers of the Mormon heretics at the end of virtually every sermon he had given over the past several months. Doing so again was, by now, something his congregation had grown to expect.

"And now, my blessed friends, I leave you with a final and parting caution. You will remember that I shared with you the fate of the Gay family after they allowed themselves to be deceived by the Mormons. They had been so worried about their son's health, that Satan was able to use this fear in order to turn them away from the gospel.

"I am afraid, my friends, that the Gay family is not alone. The terrible disease that these Mormons have brought into our valleys has spread. Barbes around the valleys tell me that as many as fifteen or twenty of our dear brothers and sisters have fallen into the traps that the Devil as laid for their destruction.

"Good people have been led astray. Hard working, honest

families. The scriptures say that even the most elect will be deceived! My dear friends, see that you protect yourselves!"

Barba Peyrot's voice was becoming very passionate. He was admonishing his people with as much force as he could muster. James had never seen him so upset. It was frightening!

"We have learned that the Mormons take women from all over the world, and bring them to a place that they call Deseret. There they force them to become the second, third, or even fourth wife of one of their barbarous men.

"Yes, they have multiple wives! All of them living! All of them slaves to one man!

"But, my friends, I do not worry about those of you here today, so much as I do about others. You are our most faithful families. You are the ones who are here even amidst the deepest snows. Indeed, those of you here today are our most elect and choice families." Barba Peyrot was speaking much more calmly now, again with a tone of kindness and love.

"No, my friends, I do not fear for you. It is others that I am concerned about. Now let us pray."

Barba Peyrot read his concluding prayer, and the

congregation then all went their separate ways, into the mountains where they would remain until warmer weather once again fought back and ultimately gained a temporary victory over winter.

January 1853

Chapter Six

Winter's Solitude

It had been too long since the sun had set, and with each passing minute Papa grew more concerned. "He is a smart lad. He knows what to do. He has been out in worse." Papa's words were offered more to appease his own troubled heart than to comfort anyone else.

As the family sat huddled under blankets, gusts of freezing wind repeatedly assaulted their home. This wind was searching the exterior of their cottage, looking for even the smallest holes through which to enter. Jean had built a fire, but it couldn't compete with the cold air that was pressing in through every crevice around them. What little heat this fire managed to create was quickly carried away in winter's relentless grasp.

"Marguerite, sweetheart, what are you doing?" called Papa, who had wandered into a neighboring room; a small area where the family prepared their meals.

"She is putting things up on the walls!" replied James, his voice colored with both curiosity and amusement.

"Decorating!" smiled Papa briefly, as he passed back through the door that separated the two rooms. "Yes, child. And won't Daniel be surprised when he returns and sees the changes that you have made."

Papa's mind had been on his middle son, who was at that moment several hours past due from a hunting excursion. However, despite this, and also despite having been separated from Marguerite by a stone wall, Papa couldn't have avoided hearing the clatter of Marguerite's chair against the floor, or the sound of her occasional complaint when something or someone inevitably got in her way.

Papa moved across the room, tenderly touching each of his children as he passed them. After making his way to the opposite side of the room, he sat down in an old wooden chair that had once belonged to James' grandfather. Papa then muttered anxiously to no one in particular, "I shouldn't have allowed him to go."

"Papa, we didn't know a storm was coming, and we need the meat," offered Jean.

"Yes, but I should have made you go with him, Jean." retorted Papa.

"He knows the area. And he *is* your son, Papa! You taught him how to hunt. He will be home soon," Jean suggested, though there was more doubt in his voice than he had intended to express.

Winter had conquered the high Alps, blanketing the family farm in several inches of snow. It was a perilously difficult season that lasted for more than half of each year, and currently held James and his family as captives. Prisoners to a jailer who cared little about the repetitiveness of their monotonous days, and even less about the state of their hungry stomachs.

Each family member worked to distract themselves as they awaited the liberation and fresh supplies that spring would bring. Tonight they had the added burden of having to also distract themselves from thinking about what might have happened to their brother.

James' oldest brother Jean spent his time reading. It was a pleasure that he rarely got to indulge in during warmer months. However, each year, as autumn weakened, and then ultimately surrendered to the onslaught of winter's determined advance, time became more abundant. Free time, which was a rare summer luxury, became winter's relentless curse. For Jean, reading became as much a hobby as a crutch, supporting his sanity.

Of course, before Jean could escape into a story, he first had to get his hands on a book. During winter, time was in plentiful abundance. Books, however, were an entirely different matter. The people of the valleys were poor, and books were an expensive luxury that few could afford. Fortunately, Europe had been kind to the Waldensians in recent years. Their meager libraries had in the last few years been greatly supplemented by donations from Switzerland and Great Britain. Generous individuals living all across Protestant Europe felt a special affection toward the Waldensian people. Those nations that had partaken in the Great Reformation did their best to honor the role of the people of the valleys. Believing, as did the Waldensians, that their role in history had been ordained by God. And now that they too carried the gospel light, these Protestants had tremendous compassion upon the people of the valleys.

By the time James had been born, more than 300 years had passed since brave reformers like Martin Luther had begun to share the burden of carrying that gospel light. Since joining them in their now shared gospel beliefs, the subsequently reformed sects of Christendom had not forgotten their once lonely alpine brothers. All across Europe, they still held the Waldensians in high regard.

And so it was, that in an effort to assist, and especially to alleviate the miserable poverty that persisted among the Waldensians, these good reformers had on several occasions taken up collections to provide basic necessities for them. Books had occasionally been among the items sent. The Waldensians showed their gratitude by devouring these treasures. So much so, that by the time a once pristine book had at last found its way into the hands of Jean, it was usually worn and tattered, having already passed under the eyes of hundreds of others.

Receiving an item in such a state of utter deterioration was not a terribly unfamiliar experience for them. Everything from their clothing to their tired cropping sickles were utilized until they became unusable. And even then, after these items had been torn to shreds, or rusted beyond repair, the family often still put these items to use, re-purposing them to some new task. Such as by converting a worn shirt into cleaning rags, or using an old piece of metal as an arrow tip.

In any event, it was not the quality of a book's binding or pages that mattered to Jean, it was the content of the stories that he cared about.

As Jean read, the broken, tattered, and stained pages faded away, leaving in their place scenes of distant and warmer climes, where the people were not held as hostages by the endless snows of a brutal mountain. These stories lifted him up and carried him away from his cold and drafty cottage. It didn't take long before Jean would become completely unaware of anything happening around him. Lost in an adventure, he became disconnected from the chatter of the rest of the family around him.

"What do you think of Marguerite's decorations, Jean?" queried Papa. "Jean! Son! . . . "

James quietly observed Papa's attempts to get his older brother's attention. Papa did not get upset or impatient with Jean. James supposed that after surviving sixty two winters, Papa understood how tedious these forced annual retreats could become.

Papa smiled and gently placed his hand on Jean's shoulder.

James had also learned how important it was that everyone find a way to hold on to their wits. Without such distractions, it didn't take long for tensions to rise and tempers to flair. Especially tonight, when a family member was missing, making everyone especially emotional.

"Jean! Look at the walls! Your sister has hung some, well . . . " Papa was careful in selecting his words. James supposed that he did not want to offend Marguerite. "She has hung some interesting . . . decorations."

Startled as much by Papa's words as by the sudden realization that he was not a character in a far away tale, but instead still stuck in their family's villa, Jean looked up and glanced around the room.

Jean slowly replied, "Marguerite, my dear, that is, err, beautiful!" He said, with as much enthusiasm as he could muster. Jean was clearly humoring his little sister. Everything from his expression to the tone of his voice made it clear that Jean was not sincere.

Not detecting the humoring tone that both Papa and Jean had employed, and which were so obvious to James, Marguerite blushed with pride.

ॐ

Daniel had hiked much farther than he had intended. But the mountain chamois he was tracking would be worth the extra time it would take to get it home. If only he could get close enough to get off an arrow.

A chamois buck would provide food for a couple of days, insuring that his family would not have to worry about how they were going to eat, at least for a little while.

Daniel worked to position himself downwind, just as Papa had taught him. He moved with stealth as he circled the beautiful animal. Close enough so that he would not lose sight of it, but far enough away so as to not startle the animal.

It was difficult to move through the snow, which was several feet deep. Papa had shown Daniel how to fashion special snowshoes using young green tree branches and leather straps. By bending the green branches into hoops, and then crisscrossing the leather straps back and forth between the two sides, a large flat disk was created. He could then tie these disks to his feet. The effect was almost magical. These snowshoes allowed Daniel to walk much more effectively and with far less effort across the surface of the snow. It was still difficult going, especially if he had to go very far, but the contraptions did allow him to move about outside. Something that would have been impossible otherwise.

Daniel's family depended on his hunting skills, and he honestly didn't mind having to spend all day looking for their next meal. In fact, when it came right down to it, he preferred being alone, with no one but the animals to keep him company. These animals didn't judge his awkwardness. They didn't expect him to be funny, or to know what to say or do in various situations. They simply scuttled about from branch to branch across the forest canopy. If one of them did happen to make Daniel uncomfortable, he could always just shoot it!

Daniel continued to think about his family, as he began his slow approach toward the unsuspecting chamois. As he drew nearer to it, he carefully reached around and over his head, pulling an arrow from his quiver. He then glided swiftly but silently forward so as to not make any noise. Just a little farther ahead and he would reach a large flat boulder. Daniel decided that this would be the perfect platform from which to shoot.

At last, after several hours of patiently stalking his prey and waiting for the right moment, it was finally now time to make the kill.

There had been moments earlier in the day when he probably could have loosed one of his arrows, but had instead chosen not to. At each of those moments, everything had not been perfect. In one of these instances he had been close enough, but his angle had been off. If he had shot at this bad angle, then the risk of missing the animal's heart was too great. It wouldn't have done his family any good if he struck the chamois anywhere besides its heart. It would still likely die, but it would run off first, perhaps several miles away, before finally falling to the ground.

Papa had taught Daniel that patience was one of the most important attributes of a good hunter. Never be in a hurry to kill your prey. If you don't have a perfect shot, then don't take it. Keep following, and eventually the opportunity to take the animal would present itself.

Daniel had spent the better part of the day tracking this animal and at last the moment had arrived. Finally, everything was right. He was down wind, he was at the right angle, the clearing was large enough that the chamois would not get lost in the thicket of trees if it took more then a dozen steps before dying, and in just a few more moments, he would be close enough.

As Daniel took his last few silent steps toward the boulder from which he planned to launch his arrow, an unexpected and rather strong gust of wind roared through the trees, frightening the chamois off.

Daniel sighed, and prepared to track it yet farther across the mountainside. He took another step when a second gust of frigid arctic air rushed through the forest, causing a nearby branch to release its collected snows directly onto Daniel's face, a large portion sliding inside the collar of Daniel's thin jacket and down onto his bare skin.

Frustrated by the poorly timed wind that had first frightened away his prey, and then had also targeted him personally with a face full of icy snow, Daniel glanced up at the sky to ask the Lord why he was being so thoroughly punished today. The view that he saw above him was startling. It was much later than he had realized, though he couldn't be sure what time it was; the sun was hidden from view by ominous-looking clouds.

When had they appeared in the sky? Daniel had been so engrossed in catching his prize that he had not noticed the changing state of the weather above him. The initial calm temperament that had welcomed in the day had since become a threatening and dangerous-looking menace. Had Daniel been paying attention, he would have headed home hours earlier. He knew better than to be out in a storm like the one that appeared to be rapidly building overhead. Many experienced mountaineers had been frozen alive in storms like these.

As Daniel began to make his way back toward his home, the winds around him gathered strength. They seemed to have decided to do everything that they could to insure that he would not be successful in his efforts to return to the family farm.

&

Although Marguerite had not noticed the patronizing tone in the voices of either Papa or Jean, to James, their attempt to hide their true feelings about her efforts at decorating the inside of their home had been painfully clear.

James watched Marguerite as she continued to pin up what Papa had generously called "decorations." To James, the dead flowers and worn cloth looked more like someone had left the window open, allowing the wind to not only carry in weeds, but also some of the dirty laundry from off the clothesline. James was not dumb enough, however, to point out this observation to Marguerite. To do so would have meant declaring war on her overly sensitive disposition. James had no desire to waste his energy in such a pursuit. At least not right now. Not while tensions were already so high. Even during easier times she was not one who forgot trespasses quickly. And as long as you remained on her bad side, or until she became distracted by some other complaint, Marguerite could be a rather unpredictable roommate. Through accidental bumps, unintentional jabs, and by serving you smaller portions at meal time, she could make life difficult. It did not pay to have her as your enemy.

Instead, James contented himself by sitting on the floor with his back against the wall, practicing a game that many of the boys in the valleys played. Taking a collection of small rounded stones which he had carefully gathered from a nearby stream, James skillfully tossed each rock across the room into a small basket that he had placed on the floor next to the opposite wall. James had become rather good at this little pastime. He could usually get almost all of the stones to hit their target, though admittedly, some occasionally did bounce back out. Still, James figured that as long as they hit the inside of the basket, they counted.

To make this amusement more challenging, James would sometimes first bounce the rocks off the wall or floor before sending them flying on a final course toward the basket. Or he would obscure his view of the basket by placing a chair between it and himself.

Tonight it was difficult to concentrate on his game. Daniel was often very severe with James, but he was still his big brother, and James was every bit as worried about Daniel's safety as he would have been if it had been Jean who was out beyond his curfew.

Gathering all his stones into the basket that Antoinette had made for him, James carefully put them on a shelf near the wall. James then walked across the room and sat down by Papa. Papa was always a good source of diversion. He knew many stories, most by heart. And he loved to share them.

Preoccupied, Papa did not speak with his usual enthusiasm. But James didn't feel guilty in pressing him for a story. He figured it was as much a diversion for Papa as it was for himself.

"Papa, tell us the story of Jean Leger," James encouraged.

Papa began slowly, but became more animated as he went along. Recounting the well known tale had a calming effect on everyone in the room.

A poor and relatively unknown barba who lived in the mid 1600s, Leger had unexpectedly found himself in the middle of one of the most violent ordeals in Waldensian history. All around him his people were being brutally murdered by a powerful and relentless army. Leger somehow managed to sneak past this army of more than 14,000 soldiers, who had been charged with the task of utterly destroying the peaceful Waldensian villages.

Hiding for two days in an icy hole, deprived of food, and with nothing to keep him warm, Leger waited until the soldiers had all passed by overhead. This pauper of no importance then miraculously, and with the providence of heaven, managed to get an audience with Oliver Cromwell himself, the mighty Lord Protector of Great Britain. There, in the court of this powerful sovereign, he convinced Cromwell to use the might of England to sue the French armies for peace on behalf of the helpless people of the valleys.

Another of James' favorite stories was that of the brave

Henri Arnaud. He loved the story in part because his best friend had been named after him. But this was not the only reason. The fact was that virtually every young man James' age grew up idolizing Arnaud.

Despite tremendous opposition from many European nations, Arnaud led an army of 900 untrained and underfed soldiers to victory against a military power that was 22,000 soldiers strong.

James and his friends would sometimes find a boulder or outcropping on the side of the mountain which they would use as a makeshift fort. There they would pretend to defend it against the French and Savoy soldiers. At length, they would claim victory for the people of the valleys and usher in what would eventually become known as the "Glorious Return."

Glorious, because no one thought it was possible. The Waldensians had at that time been recently driven from their valleys into the protective arms of the Protestant nations of Europe. These countries opened their arms and homes to the Waldensians, encouraging them to become permanent residents. The Protestants reasoned with them that a return to their mountains would be impossible; they were at that time occupied by the largest military force that Europe had seen in generations.

At first the Waldensian people tried to build new lives. But they struggled to adjust. Like eagles, longing for their high perches, the people of the mountains could think of nothing but returning to their homes. Even a large merciless army was not sufficient to soften their determination.

It was in this moment that Henri Arnaud and his tiny army left on their impossible mission, somehow managing to defeat a force that outnumbered them more than twenty to one. These brave defenders of the Lord's chosen people cleared the way for their homesick brothers and sisters to return. However great the victory, the spirit of this people was forever altered.

As a reminder of their having been forced from their lands, it had since become the tradition of the people to not overly invest in their abodes. Decorating their homes seemed an almost pointless activity. They viewed these buildings as nothing more than extensions of the land around them, a part of the very mountainside. History had taught them that a house could be lost in an instant and without warning. At any time, powerful armies from outside their community might once again enter their valleys and force them into the caves or crevices of the higher mountains.

Why invest in decor when you may not live in the building tomorrow?

Which is why Marguerite's efforts to decorate the walls of their drab surroundings seemed to the rest of the family to be out of place. But if it kept her occupied, then it meant that she would not be complaining about being too cold, or about having to fix another meal, or about any number of other things that she found terribly unfair. Having the walls covered with weeds and laundry was far less of a burden than trying to tune out her many discontented comments.

After Papa finished his stories, he sighed, saying, "I am going to get some more firewood." He stood and headed for the neatly stacked wood next to the fireplace. "When Daniel gets home he is going to be cold. Let's see if we can't get this house a little warmer for him."

Their home had stood since the late 1600s, when it had been built by James' Great-Great-Grandfather. And although it was old, it was still very solid. This two-story structure was made almost entirely out of stone, topped off with a roof made from giant slabs of slate. These were laid one on top of the other, ascending toward the pitch, making the house waterproof.

As Papa worked to build up the fire, James sought the comfort of his oldest sister Antoinette. If he sat close enough to her, then she would rub his back or play with his hair. If, for some reason, she didn't start doing this on her own, James knew that if he placed his head on her knee, she would soon start.

"Antoinette, will you sing me a song?" James asked. Antoinette loved music, and as a result, so did James. Indeed, music was among the very few unbroken and unworn things that James got to enjoy. It didn't matter how poor you were, music was free. It could be enjoyed equally by kings as well as by poor alpine mountaineers. James continued to rest his head on Antoinette's lap listening as her soft voice gently floated down, enjoying both the music, and the sensation of her fingers running through his hair.

Although they could not afford to buy instruments, Antoinette had still managed to teach herself to read music. A skill that she had patiently worked to pass along to James. Antoinette had been thrilled that James seemed to be so enthusiastic about their music lessons. For James, it gave him something that he could share with his sister. She had also tried to teach Daniel to read music, but these efforts had not ended successfully; the concepts seemed to simply refuse to take up lodging in Daniel's head. After repeating the same drills over and over, Daniel had eventually become so frustrated that he swore that he would never pick up a sheet of music again. True to his word, he had entirely avoided the subject since.

$\wp$

Daniel was grateful that he knew the mountain as well as he did. It was now completely impossible to see more than a few feet in any direction. If he hadn't known the individual trees so well, he might not have been able to continue traveling toward his home. He certainly could not rely on the distant mountain peaks to give him his bearings since they were obscured from view by thick clouds and by the circling snows that now surrounded him, filling the air.

Daniel was miserable. He couldn't remember a time when he had ever been so intolerably cold. His clothing was not particularly warm to begin with, but tonight he was not just under-dressed, he was also wet. Daniel cursed himself for being so foolish. It was his own fault that he was in such a difficult predicament.

The sun was now setting and the temperature was beginning to plunge rapidly. Daniel wondered what would happen to his family should he not survive the night. Who would provide food for them? And without food, how would they eat? The meat that Daniel brought home was not just a welcome blessing, it was a life-sustaining necessity for his family. Daniel feared that his thoughtlessness would not only cost him his own life, but would also put his family in danger.

With a great distance still to travel, Daniel's pace began to slacken. His fingers, toes, and ears ached, while his face burned. The rest of his body complained from an unhappy combination of being everywhere wet and cold. The effort that it took to continue moving toward his home grew steadily greater.

Daniel thought about his family. When he was not out hunting, he sometimes attempted to join in their conversations. These awkward attempts at bonding were not typically successful. He knew that his family cherished him, but he just didn't quite understand how to relate to them. His humor usually ended up sounding like insults, while his requests often came off like the commands of a general. For reasons that Daniel could not grasp, when he played with James, his younger brother usually ran away in tears.   Eventually, out of both frustration and complete bafflement at the inner-workings of others, Daniel typically just ended up pulling back into himself.

As he found himself alone, his strength quickly draining away by the effort it took to walk through the deep snow and against the howling wind, Daniel was surprised to realize that he regretted not trying harder to understand his family.   This realization caused him to begin to hurt inside.   Not just from the cold, but also because he might die without ever getting to tell his family that he loved them.

"Lord, please don't let me die," he quietly uttered through frozen and chapped lips.   "Not until I can let my family know how much I love them."   Daniel then collapsed into a pile of soft snow.

∽

It had been several hours since anyone had said anything. James was only thirteen years old, but he was no fool.   He knew that it would be almost impossible for his brother to survive a night like this outside alone.   As the night mercilessly marched along, the odds that Daniel was still alive became less and less favorable.

Suddenly, in a voice that betrayed exasperation, Jean jumped up and loudly stated, "Enough sitting here. I am going to go find him!"

Papa placed his age worn hand on Jean's shoulder, "You are strong, but it would be an unwise errand. I cannot . . . " Papa choked on his words, "I need you here, son."

A few more hours of silence then another unexpected sound; something banging loudly against the downstairs door. James suspected that the banging had been nothing more than one of the cattle kicking the door with its hooves. However, regardless of this likelihood, James hurried down the stairs nonetheless.

Like all the people of the upper mountains, James' family kept their animals inside their home during the colder months. It was the custom of their people to build their homes so that the bottom floor could function, when needed, as a stable. They did this to conserve both the warmth of the animals, and also that of themselves. By combining the natural warmth of both the animals and people in the same building, less fuel was needed to keep all of them alive.

James arrived at the bottom of the stairs and glanced about the room. He did not see any of the animals out of place. Again, he hard a loud BANG BANG BANG, clearly it was coming from the front door. James pulled open the large wooden door that protected them from the outside and was immediately pelted by a ridged arctic blast. The animals around him recoiled to the opposite side of the single downstairs room.

"Begging your pardon, but may we please come in?" yelled a slightly chubby man, trying to speak loudly enough so as to be heard over the wind. A second man stood near to the one that was speaking.

"We are too far from our home and don't dare attempt to get any closer in this blizzard!"

James gestured for them to come in. The two men walked forward, and James promptly closed the door behind them. As they entered, the light of James' candle revealed that a third man was with them as well. The two men he had initially noticed were helping this third man who could not stand on his own.

"We found him outside. Nearly froze to death, poor fellow. Do you know him?" asked one of the men.

It was then that James realized who the men had carried in with them. He squealed with involuntary delight, "Papa! He's home! Papa!"

Papa came running down the stairs, skipping several steps at the bottom. "Daniel, my dear boy! Thank you for bringing my son home to me!" he choked through his tears.

"Antoinette! Jean! Help me get Daniel into dry clothes. James, go and fetch a hot stone from the fire and some blankets. Marguerite, heat up some water and make a broth."

Watching Papa work over his unresponsive older brother was both terrifying and comforting to James. "Will he be okay, Papa?" James timidly asked.

"He is alive, and with the Lord's help, we will keep him that way," Papa replied.

After several minutes of labor in his behalf, Daniel lay in dry clothing near the fire, wrapped in bundles of blankets with a hot stone from the fire placed carefully inside to help warm him up. His irregular breathing was frightening. James had never seen his older brother look so defenseless.

One of their visitors cautiously spoke, "Pardon our intrusion, sir, on your family, but we are ministers of the Lord Jesus Christ. We hold his priesthood. Would you allow us to give the lad a blessing of healing?"

James had forgotten that the two strangers were in their home. He didn't know what they meant by "a blessing of healing." Were they referring to the same kind of blessing that Joseph Gay had been given? The kind of blessing that the barbes had forbidden? If a blessing of healing would save his brother, like it had helped the three year old Gay boy, then James didn't care what anyone else thought— he wanted his brother to have it.

James was grateful that Papa seemed to agree. "The Lord led you to him when he lay helpless in the snow. I will not now turn you away when you also offer to leave a blessing upon his head. If you say that you are ministers, then please, go ahead and minister to him."

1853

Chapter Seven

A Fallen Brother

In the solitude of the mountains, your survival or failure was entirely dependent upon yourself. It was not that your neighbors were unwilling to help, they did so whenever they could. But their equally impoverished condition meant that they couldn't very easily lift you onto higher ground than that which they themselves were standing upon. Each year as winter's bitter hand took hold of the landscape, the importance of this self-sufficiency became all the more evident.

During this difficult season, heavy snows cut the many

families of the mountains off from all but their nearest neighbors. This made calling upon each other an infrequent and ill-advised activity. The energy necessary to traverse the mountainside forced the would-be guest to give additional consideration to the wisdom of such a trek.

It was in this lonesome setting that Papa did all that he could to improve Daniel's condition. One of the blessings of self-sufficiency was that you learned a variety of useful skills. Knowing how to care for one's own sick being among these.

More than a week had passed since Daniel had returned home. The ministers who had found him remained in lodging with the family, and supplies were running lower than ever. However, these men did not create an additional burden. Instead, they had proved to be indispensable. The older of the two, Barthélémy Pons, was Waldensian. He had spent his long life surviving similarly difficult conditions, and was well versed in the skills needed to survive in the mountains. Barthélémy had spent the week chopping and stacking firewood, hunting, and helping Jean with repairs to their home.

The younger man was not from the valleys. James learned that Jabez Woodard had traveled to the Waldensian Alps from

London a year earlier.

Having spent most of his life in a more civilized part of the world, Jabez was not nearly as adept at living off the land as were the rest of the group. But what he lacked in experience, he more than made up for in his work ethic, and even more so in his ability to cook.

Using the same sparse ingredients at each meal, Jabez somehow managed to create a new and wonderfully different dish for them to enjoy. To James, Marguerite seemed to act utterly muddle-headed whenever Jabez was around. She appeared to be taken by both his culinary gifts as well as by his good looks and charming personality.

Over the years, each member of the family had acquired responsibility for certain chores, either because they had a knack for a specific task, or in Marguerite's case, because they were not good at anything else. Marguerite was responsible for cooking the family meals. She despised the job. She was also not very good at it. But cooking saved her from having to do many of the outside chores, where she was more likely to get dirty or sweaty.

Marguerite's meals were edible, but they were unimaginative and lacked variety. Something that struck James as odd. Marguerite could add so much color and variety to her apparel, but seemed unable to come up with the slightest variation on the meals she cooked. Every morning they ate the same bland bread. The menu for supper and dinner depended in large part on what meat Daniel was able to provide. That meat was cooked thoroughly and served in a fashion that was safe enough to eat, though often without any side items. Or if side items were included, they were always as an afterthought, and as such, poorly prepared.

Of course, James knew that there were few supplies. Perhaps he was being unfair to Marguerite. How many ways could she arrange the same few and limited ingredients that were available to her? Still, James found it difficult to eat the same thing day after day, and often wished that the family could have a better cook.

James supposed that Marguerite wished that the family could have a different cook as well. And for these few brief weeks, both her and James' desires were being fulfilled. Jabez spent much of his time preparing meals for the group. Marguerite's assignment as family cook gave her a convenient excuse to spend time with the stranger, something that she took advantage of. Jabez tolerated her flirtations with gentlemanly kindness, but was careful not to return them. Whenever she was near, Jabez spoke frequently of his young wife and two children, and of how much he loved and missed them. Marguerite, however, never seemed to catch the hint.

James was embarrassed by what he believed to be the foolish way that Marguerite presented herself to Jabez. Still, he did appreciate the fact that at least with Jabez around, Marguerite's complaints had grown less frequent. Having Barthélémy and Jabez taking care of the morning and mealtime chores left the family better able to focus on helping Daniel, who had had a rough week.

Daniel slept long hours, waking only long enough to eat and take care of personal needs. He would then collapse back into his pile of blankets and fall back into a deep sleep. His family worked hard to keep him warm and comfortable.

To James, Daniel had always been frighteningly large and terrifyingly powerful; stronger than many of their full grown adult neighbors. James had believed that no one across the entire mountainside could have subjected his brother to their will. Most were not strong enough. Those who might have had the strength lacked the determination that Daniel had. They might get the best of him on the first few blows, but they would soon find Daniel to be relentless, like a mountain goat, hitting the same spot over and over again, looking for weaknesses. Daniel would have struck back repeatedly until the aggressor cried out for peace. Even then, it would have been some time before Daniel relented. Not until he grew tired of the sport.

No one, other than perhaps Papa himself, could outwork Daniel. Jean worked hard, but his build and frame simply did not allow him to get as much done. James was much smaller than either of them. He did the best he could to keep up with his older brothers, but at the end of the day, he inevitability had done far less work than either of them had.

Daniel always picked the toughest tasks. Those jobs that would require hours of hard labor, such as digging tree stumps out of the crop field, or hauling rocks from the crops fields out to the mountainside. Jobs that everyone else was glad to let him do. With impressive perseverance, he could work all day long without complaint, his large, tanned muscles glistening with sweat in the sunlight.

It was difficult for James to see his brother now lying next to the fire, crumpled up in a defenseless pile on the floor. If Daniel could succumb to such humiliating weakness, then anyone could.

James remembered all the times that Daniel had bullied him. He thought about how he had often chosen to walk the long way home in order to avoid a confrontation with Daniel. And now, here lay his older brother before him, unable to so much as lift his head for more than a few brief moments.

James thought about all the times he had wanted revenge against Daniel. The many times he had wished that he were the stronger brother so that he could teach Daniel a lesson. It was ironic to James now that his opportunity had come, now that he was indeed the stronger of the two, all he wanted to do was care for Daniel, and to see him get better.

As frightening as Daniel could be when he was at his strongest, seeing him in this weakened state was much more terrifying. James had often despised his older brother. He had even feared him. But he had never imagined how much he loved him.

Somewhere during the last week, as Daniel lay before them, alternating between shivering and sweating, his breathing erratic and irregular, James had begun to fear that he might lose Daniel. The thought of losing him was unbearable to James. To think that his tough ox of an older brother might not be there in the spring to help work the farm was a thought that James could not fathom.

With each passing day James' apprehension grew. Why wasn't Daniel improving? It had been too long. Surely he should be getting better by now. Each morning James leapt out of bed and rushed to where Daniel lay in search of some sign of improvement. This morning was no different.

"How is he today, Papa?" James managed through a tired yawn.

"Come here, my boy," Papa gestured toward James with an outstretched arm.

James slid to the other side of Daniel and sat next to Papa on a wooden bench made from an old fallen log, which had been split down the middle, creating a flat surface to sit on.

"You are a good boy, James," Papa said encouragingly, as he wrapped his large arm around James, resting his hand on the top of James'.

"Do you know why we named your brother Daniel?"

Daniel had always carried the name that he did. It was who he was. He was Daniel. James had never considered that Papa and Mama might have selected his name for any specific purpose.

James shook his head.

"Remember, James, the story of Daniel from the Bible?"

James nodded. He had been taught the story of Daniel and the lions' den. It was one of his favorite stories. Daniel had been a faithful prophet, who loved to pray. The king of the land where Daniel lived ordered that anyone who prayed should be thrown into a pit of lions to be devoured. At the risk of his own life, Daniel persevered in his duty to pray to God. He was cast into the pit, but was miraculously protected from harm by the Lord.

"When Daniel was born, your mother and I felt that he was a very special soul. From the moment he first drew breath, he seemed to us to be a strong and determined individual," Papa smiled.

"Like Daniel of old, he had great personal strength." Papa paused, and wiped a tear from his cheek. He turned toward James, looking him directly in the eyes before continuing. "Your brother is still strong, James. He will make it through this. Don't worry. Perhaps the Lord is testing him. Perhaps he is testing all of us. But James, my boy, I feel it in my heart. Daniel will be alright."

The conviction in Papa's voice was palpable. So much so, that it greatly helped to ease James' mind. If Papa believed that

James would be alright, then he would be.

Over the next few days, Daniel's condition grew much worse. His fever deepened, and the color of his skin turned a horrible shade of pale white. Daniel's brief moments of consciousness decreased until he was not waking up at all. Despite their best efforts, the family was unable to get him to drink anything. They feared that if they forced him to drink, he may accidentally inhale the water, and drown.

The comfort that Papa had spoken to James' heart a few days earlier was quickly eroding away. Even Papa now seemed less certain of Daniel's fate. The house felt like a solemn, quiet sanctuary. The desperation and despair hung so thick in the air that James was sure that even the animals downstairs could feel it.

It was on the evening of the eighth day that Jabez Woodard addressed Papa as the family prepared to eat their supper. "Jean, I think we ought to fast for Daniel."

"What is fasting?" James asked Jabez.

"It is a principal of the gospel that allows man to more directly call upon the powers of heaven for special blessings," Jabez answered.

Papa smiled at Jabez, "Yes, that is a unique idea. A fast . . ." Papa's voice trailed off.

Jabez continued, "Jean, if you will allow me, I will offer a prayer. We will then all abstain from eating any food for the next full day."

Papa nodded.

"Dear Father in Heaven, please bless this lad that he might be fully healed according to the priesthood blessing that he received, and according to the faith of his family. A faith that they are willing to demonstrate through this fast, which we all now enter into."

Abstain from food? Wondered James. Did Jabez mean to suggest that they not eat? But, thought James, supper was already prepared, and he was famished. A meal lay before them which Jabez had already made. The house was filled with the aroma of savory squirrel meat. It smelled so good. Even better now, it seemed, than it had before Jabez had suggested the unusual idea that they not eat it.

James could not remember the barbes ever preaching about fasting, though Papa seemed to know what fasting was, so he supposed it must have been a true gospel principal. If it would help to open the doors of heaven and bless Daniel's recovery, then James decided that he was willing to try it.

Before they had begun their fast, the food on the table had just been another meal. Now it proved to be a great temptation. The family could not afford to waste the food. It would have to remain there in the same room with them, on the table, just a few feet away, dripping with flavor. James' stomach growled all night as he thought about the cooked meat that lay on the table, waiting to be eaten.

Throughout the next day, it took all the will power James could muster to keep himself from eating. James was used to living on small rations, but this was different. This was the first time that he had ever had to not eat when food was not only available, but cooked. When all he had to do was reach out his hand and pick the food up. He couldn't even go outside to avoid thinking about eating. He was forced to sit all day, staring at the meal that he was not allowed to touch.

Papa did not force any of them to fast. James knew that if he wanted to, he could eat. No one would have looked down on him or said anything. A few times throughout the day he seriously considered doing exactly that. After all, he was the youngest. No one expected him to be as strong as the rest of them. They would all pat him on the back, and tell him that he had done his best, and that it was okay that he had not made it the entire day.

The thought of being patronized for being weak and for giving in quickly brought James' resolve back to its full strength. He was not about to let the rest of them think he was weaker than they were. If they could endure the trial of fasting, then so could he.

That evening, Barthélémy Pons offered a second prayer. This time, one of thanksgiving. He once again asked the Lord to bless Daniel, and ended their fast. The group then ate the meal that Jabez had prepared the day before. James thought that it tasted better than just about anything he had ever eaten.

Another day passed without any improvement on Daniel's part. The faith of everyone in the room was tried to the very limits. Everyone, even Marguerite, who was usually too busy thinking about herself to notice anyone else, was quiet and sullen.

Then, with little notice the following morning, just after the sun rose, Daniel unexpectedly sat up, surprising everyone in the room. Stretching his arms out above his head, as though he were waking up from a short Sunday nap, Daniel looked around at everyone and sleepily commented, "Good morning," as he yawned loudly. Not realizing that anything was out of the ordinary, Daniel asked, "Did I oversleep?"

As the tension that had hung in the air for more than a week and a half suddenly burst like a soap bubble, everywhere in the room, both family and guest erupted into a mixture of laughter and tears.

"Yes, my boy, you overslept," smiled Papa, as he gently placed his hand on Daniel's back.

Several minutes passed in celebration. The family knelt together and Papa gave thanks to their God that Daniel had been preserved. As Daniel observed this scene, the confusion caused by too much sleep and too little food began to wear off from his strained mind, allowing the memory of his ill-fated trek through the mountainside to return to his awareness.

"Papa," he whispered, "I am sorry."

From that point forward, Daniel's recovery progressed rapidly. His appetite was ravenous. He had gone several days on very little to no food. Now that he was once again eating, Daniel consumed twice as much food as any of the rest of them. No one seemed to mind, though. It was such a relief to have him back that everyone else was more than happy to eat a little less so that Daniel could continue to get his strength back.

As Daniel's physical condition improved, something remained different about him. There was something that James could not quite put his finger on that was altered in Daniel. He was the same young man. Still tough. Still strong. But somehow James felt more comfortable around him. He was less intimidating. James supposed that seeing Daniel in such a weakened state had made him more human. It was hard to be afraid of someone whom you had watched nearly die. Like seeing a dangerous animal injured on the side of the mountain cliffs. Instead of fearing it, you begin to pity the beast.

Daniel's large stature began to feel safer to James than it ever had before. His strength meant protection rather than danger. His love of wrestling was still as much a part of Daniel's personality as ever before, but to James, being pinned to the floor by his laughing brother now felt like an expression of love rather than a demonstration of dominance.

James waited for Daniel to say or do something characteristic of his usual blunt forcefulness. At first, James expected Daniel to grab him, throw him out into the snow, or order

James to fetch an item that he was too lazy to get himself.

When Daniel was not off hunting, he was still rough. More than once he sneaked up on James and grabbed him from behind. Stuck helpless in Daniel's grasp, James could hardly breathe as his brother squeezed the air out of his lungs. But in each of these cases, Daniel had not held onto James for long. He let him go when James asked to be released. He then patted James on the back or shoulder before walking off.

Weeks passed and still Daniel remained a more refined version of himself. He still occasionally had his awkward moments, but these were brief and becoming less common.

Most unexpected of all were Daniel's invitations for James to go hunting with him. Daniel had never before asked James to join him on a hunt. When the two had been younger, Papa had once encouraged Daniel to bring James along. At this request, Daniel had complained that James was too loud and too stupid to go hunt. His feelings hurt, James had reacted by yelling that hunting was the only thing Daniel was good at. That it was Daniel who was too stupid to do anything that required brains.

At first, James declined his invitations. He was afraid that once the two of them were alone, Daniel's abusive nature would return.   However, as the weeks wore on, James grew more comfortable with his older brother, until one day he accepted the offer.

As it turned out, Daniel had been right. James was too loud and too stupid to hunt. But to James' relief, Daniel did not point this out to him. Instead, he simply reminded James over and over again that he was walking too loudly, or that he was holding his bow incorrectly, or of any number of other errors that he made.

James was amazed at the skill that hunting required, and at how effective Daniel was at it. You could not simply go out into the forest, let an arrow fly, and expect it to land in the heart of an animal. It took hours of work. You had to know how the animals thought. You had to be able to read their tracks, and outsmart them.

In the morning of his first outing with Daniel, James spotted a rabbit. Daniel encouraged James not to shot at it, saying that they were too far away, and that he would miss. Frustrated and impatient, James determined that he would prove Daniel wrong. He pulled out an arrow, took aim, and hit a rock about ten feet away from the rabbit. The loud thump and snap of the arrow against the boulder startled their prey, causing it to dart off across the mountainside and out of sight.

As the day progressed, James attempted several other shots, hitting more boulders, a tree, and the ground. Daniel did not tease him or make fun of his inability to do anything right. James could tell that he was frustrated, but Daniel held his tongue nonetheless. And despite his ruining their hunting trip, to James' astonishment, Daniel invited him out again.

Daniel was gentler, kinder. In many ways, more like Jean. No, James thought. Not like Jean. That was not the right comparison. Jean was kind, that was true. But he was also reserved. This kinder version of Daniel was still loud and bullish. James tried to work out who Daniel had become. Who did he remind him of? He was kind, but not quiet. He was tough, but he no longer used his strength to get his way.

The biggest change, though, was in the way that Daniel communicated with the rest of his family. Where he used to try too hard to think of things to say, he now didn't try at all. And as a result, it seemed to James that Daniel began to fit in.

1853

Chapter Eight

A Precious Book

It wasn't until early spring that James finally understood what had happened to his older brother. James was still a lousy hunter but he was getting better. He had at last learned to trust Daniel's instincts. James no longer shot off arrows at every branch that blew in the wind.

James had still not managed his first kill, but he had learned to walk alongside his brother without frightening the animals away. He had learned to be patient and to quietly creep along the mountain ridges for hours on end, waiting for the opportunity to make a kill. And James had learned the most important lesson of all: If the family was going to get any supper, then he had better let Daniel be the one to shoot. Because if James did, he was sure to miss.

James practiced his aim by shooting arrows toward a dead tree behind their home. He spent hours back there, determined to improve his skill. Occasionally Daniel would walk by and give him advice or encouragement.

"You are doing great, James! You are getting better. You almost hit the tree that time!" Daniel would tease. "Here, let me show you." Daniel effortlessly launched three arrows in rapid succession, hitting the tree dead center each time.

Daniel's teasing was different than it had once been. It was not merciless. It was not mean. Instead, his comments were colored with brotherly love. This love began to cement a bond between them.

"I was aiming for the air beside the tree," James retorted. "There was a moth flying there!" James smiled.

"Yes, and I am sure that you hit it, little brother!" chortled Daniel.

While James still needed a lot more practice before he

would be a successful hunter, there was another way that he could contribute to the family's supply of meat. Today, Daniel would be taking James fishing.

The air was still cold in the upper mountains, and there was still quite a bit of snow on the ground. However, the snows had melted back enough that it was now possible for the two brothers to walk greater distances without too much effort.

It took a few hours for them to walk from the family farm to the Angrogna River. They carried homemade fishing rods that they had fashioned from straight chestnut branches and twine. As they walked, Daniel described the mechanics of fishing to James.

"Like hunting, fishing also requires patience, James. Don't expect to catch anything right away. Sometimes I fish all day and only get a few bites."

Daniel went on to instruct James that they could talk more than they did when they hunted, so long as they did so quietly.

James and Daniel arrived at the banks of the Angrogna River, and began to walk along side of it. Daniel explained that they were looking for a bend in the river; an alcove where fish were likely to hide. He explained that the fish did not like the fast moving current, and that the few that found themselves caught up in this current were not likely to be looking to nibble on anything. What they needed was a place where the waters were calm. After several minutes of walking, they found the perfect spot. As the river curved around the mountain, it had cut a cove back behind the main river. Protected on three sides from the rushing currents, the waters of this cove hardly moved at all.

Daniel pointed out a large dead tree that had fallen into the cove. He explained to James that the branches of this tree would undoubtedly be a home to many fish that would use them as a protection from predators.

Daniel instructed James to clear the snow from a nearby patch of dirt, then showed him how to dig in the ground for worms. "We will use these worms to catch the fish, unless you want to eat one first." He laughed, throwing a chubby worm at James' face.

After they had collected a number of plump, wet worms, the two young men baited their hand carved wooden hooks and cast their lines toward the dead tree.

It didn't take long before James had caught his first fish. James found that he enjoyed fishing. He was good at it. He caught a second fish, and then a third, before Daniel had even caught his first.

By afternoon, the two of them had collected eleven fish. Before heading home, they would have to gut and prepare them so they would be ready to be cooked by Marguerite.

James had helped Daniel clean his prey numerous times by now. Daniel had taught him various tricks, such as how to remove the craw from a bird, or how to skin small mammals.

These were his first fish, but the process was not all unlike that of cleaning other animals. If anything, it proved to be easier. James was being careful to insure that the fish's meat would not be contaminated by its internals. As he concentrated on the task, Daniel reached out and placed his hand on the back of James' neck, "Good work, James! I couldn't have done it better myself."

The way Daniel spoke suddenly brought the issue of who Daniel had become into focus for James. In every way, Daniel had sounded like Papa. His voice, his tone, the words that he had selected, all of them could have just as easily come out of Papa's mouth. Indeed, if he had been there with them, James would have not even looked up. He would have been absolutely certain that it had been Papa who had been speaking.

But Papa was not with them. James looked up at his

brother and saw in his eyes the same pride that Papa had bestowed upon him many times. Daniel not only sounded like his Papa, but he was sincere. He was not putting on an act, or trying to be someone that he was not. He had spoken from his heart. He probably didn't even realize how much his comments had resembled those of Papa.

Whatever had happened to Daniel that night when he had been alone in the mountains had changed him from an awkward and confused boy into a man. But not just any man. He had become a man like Papa.

Daniel had taken on the persona of James' dear Papa. It seemed an unlikely change to James. How could anyone make such a rapid conversion? How could anyone go from being the meanest person in the valleys one day, to being like the wisest man in the valleys the next? But then, thought James, perhaps these traits had always been there. Perhaps they had been clouded over by youthful inexperience. Or perhaps Daniel had become mean when Mama had died. James wondered if she had lived longer, if Daniel's temperament might have been friendlier all along.

Whatever the case may have been, James was certain of the outcome. Several weeks had now passed since Daniel had awoken from his illness. James had spent enough time with him to be sure that the change was permanent. If he was going to revert to his grumpier self, then he surely would have done so by now. Especially considering all the frustrating moments that the two had spent together, as time after time, James had ruined yet another killing opportunity by forgetting to do something that Daniel had told him ten times previously to do.

If he had managed to hold on to his more peaceful demeanor during all of these daily mishaps on James' part, then it was unlikely that he would ever regress.

The realization that Daniel was behaving like Papa stunned James. James had always loved Jean, who had never been unkind to him. Jean had never teased James, nor forced him to wrestle. But Jean was a quieter soul, less outgoing than Papa.

As James and Daniel walked home James carried their freshly gutted fish in a sack over his shoulder. James began to wonder if Papa had ever been like Daniel. Had a younger version of Papa been ornery? Had he been awkward? Had Papa made his younger brothers wrestle? To James, it seemed a strange thing to consider. Papa was too kind, too good. And yet, the thought could not be avoided. The evidence presented itself before James on a daily basis in the form of a reformed, Papa-like Daniel.

As the mountainside continued to warm and spring began to turn into summer, Barthélémy Pons and Jabez Woodard were frequent visitors at the family farm.

The experience that they had weathered together had formed a bond between them. In time, Barthélémy brought his wife and children to meet James' family.

It was Sunday. The five members of the Pons family had spent the early part of their Sabbath day visiting with neighbors at the nearby Cardon family farm. Barthélémy explained to Papa that after they had finished at the Cardon Farm, he had decided that he wanted to introduce his wife and children to his new friends. They then had all made the trek together, walking across the mountain trails to James' family farm, arriving just after noon.

"Jean, I am pleased to introduce to you my dear wife, Marie." Barthélémy beamed with pride. "She is a dear woman, and a blessing to our little family."

"And these are our three children. David is our eldest."

David was a skinny sort of fellow who, although not strong, was nevertheless gifted when it came to working with his hands.

In time, James learned that David could fix just about anything. He was also a very lighthearted soul, full of life and quick-witted. He frequently made comments that showed an intelligent sense of humor.

"And this is our oldest daughter, Lydia." Barthélémy smiled, gesturing to a tall skinny girl standing by the woman who Barthélémy had introduced as his wife.

"And finally, this here is our youngest daughter, whom we named after her mother. I love her mama so much that I could think of no prettier name for a new born baby girl." Barthélémy smiled and winked at his wife.

Lydia and Marie were beautiful enough to catch Marguerite's attention, but not so pretty as to make her dislike them.

Marie, who was about six months younger than Marguerite, developed an almost immediate affection for James' older sister. When alone, Marie was a sensible enough girl. But whenever she was around Marguerite she seemed to lose herself in a pursuit to impress her new friend.

Lydia Pons, who was four years older than Marie, was also soft spoken, like her younger sister, but she was more self-assured.

Something that James supposed came with age and experience.

The ten of them, including both James' family and the Pons family, all sat together outside on the shady side of the family home. A few of them, including Papa, Barthélémy and his wife Marie, rested themselves upon mismatched logs that sat next to the house. Marie and Marguerite flopped themselves down in the tall grass, spreading their dresses out around them. James sat himself down on the ground with his back leaning against the family home. He then glanced up and noticed that his older brother Jean was fetching an additional log for Lydia. Jean then assisted Lydia as she sat down.

"Thank you," Lydia quietly blushed.

"Which temple do you attend?" Marguerite directed her question to the young Miss Marie Pons.

After a brief moment of uncomfortable silence, Barthélémy offered an answer. "We don't go to temple anymore, my dear Marguerite. We worship the Lord outside." Barthélémy paused, "We take turns hosting Sunday services at the homes of some of our neighbors."

What a strange way to worship, thought James. Why would anyone hold church services outside? Centuries ago, the

Waldensians had of course done exactly that. But it was out of necessity that they had done so. It was because they had been too poor to build churches. Now, with temples littering the mountains, it seemed strange to James that anyone would choose to meet outside when they didn't have to do so.

"We belong to a church called 'The Church of Jesus Christ of Latter-Day Saints.' Although many call us Mormons." Barthélémy paused, looking around to see what their reaction would be to the news that they were Mormons.

By now, everyone in the valleys had heard of the Mormons. The barbes had made sure of that. In every temple, the people had frequently been warned to keep their distance from these deceivers, as they had been labeled. The barbes had warned them that if given half the chance, the Mormons would pounce on even the most faithful Waldensians and destroy their faith in the gospel, leading them carefully away to hell.

These people did not appear to James to be devils or even devilish. Perhaps this was because they were still Waldensian at heart. Perhaps, thought James, only their leaders were evil, while those who followed them were just deceived. Still, James worried about the wisdom of keeping company with them. What if their loss of faith was indeed contagious, as the barbes seemed to think it was? What if this blasphemy spread to a member of James' family?

"We are still Waldensian, but on Sundays we worship with a small group of people, under the direction of Jabez Woodard," Barthélémy explained.

According to Barthélémy, Jabez Woodard was the leader of these Mormons. That didn't make any sense at all to James. Jabez was, of course, no stranger to James and his family. They knew him well. They had spent many weeks together recently. Jabez was a kindhearted, hard working man. If he was the leader of the Mormons then, according to the barbes, Jabez was supposed to be a vile, horrible man. He was supposed to be Satan's very servant, sent to the valleys to destroy the people of God. But James knew that Jabez Woodard was none of these things. He was a good man. Who had been willing to work hard all winter long to help James and his family survive. He had been one of the men, along with Barthélémy Pons, who had rescued his brother from a certain death.

James wondered if the barbes had ever met Jabez. If they had, how could they say such wildly untrue things about him? Or perhaps, thought James, perhaps there are still higher up leaders in the Mormon Church that the barbes were speaking of. Perhaps, like the Pons family, Jabez was not a deceiver, but was instead also among the deceived. Surely Jabez is not a wicked man, thought James. He must have instead been somehow blinded by these Mormons.

Barthélémy continued their discussion of the Mormons, explaining that they numbered about twenty five souls in the valleys. A number that was growing every month. There was, of course, Jabez Woodard, as well as Barthélémy and his family. Additional members included a small family by the name of Cardon that had just recently joined the group. Also the Malan family, the Beus family, and a few other single individuals.

These roughly twenty five individuals were spread across all three of the Waldensian valleys, making it difficult for them to spend much time together other than during their Sunday services.

Barthélémy then invited Papa to attend these services. "Jean, you and your family can come as our guests. You can sit with us," smiled Barthélémy.

Papa graciously declined the invitation in a manner that did not cast any disparaging feelings upon the Pons family or their faith. James appreciated the way his Papa had handled the situation. He had not insulted them or made them feel uncomfortable. He had wisely declined to attend their misguided services, while still managing to hold on to their friendship. James thought that this was very important.

James decided that avoiding them might protect his own family, but it would do nothing to help the Pons. How could they help their new friends find their way back into the arms of worship amongst the Waldensians if they insulted them or cut off all contact with them? James was certain that many of his neighbors would have done exactly that. Upon learning that an acquaintance had been infected by Mormonism, they would have slammed the door of friendship shut, insuring that these poor lost souls would remain lost forever. Not his Papa. James supposed that Papa too recognized that the only way to help the Pons family back was to keep fostering a relationship with them.

While Papa had declined their offer to attend the Mormon's Sunday services, he did, however, accept a generous gift that Barthélémy had offered him. A few weeks after bringing his family to their farm, Barthélémy returned once again. This time with only with his eldest son David.

"Jean, I have something I would like for you to have,"

Barthélémy said to Papa. "It is a book that has become very special to our family."

As Barthélémy handed the book to Papa, James' eyes lit up. He had never seen a book in such pristine condition before. The binding was solid, the cover was not yet frayed, the pages were white and unsoiled. James wondered how Barthélémy had obtained a book in such good repair. Even more, he wondered why Barthélémy would give something so valuable away. If James had owned a book that nice, he would never give it up.

"Jean, this is more than just a book. It contains scriptures from an ancient people that inhabited the Americas," continued Barthélémy. "I ask only that you read it."

1853

Chapter Nine

Conversion

As June marched on, the new, beautifully bound book that Barthélémy had given Papa often drew James' gaze. Mostly because it was so out of place in their home. It was the only thing that did not look utterly worn out. It stood out like a brand new gown hung in a pig pen. And at least for now, it looked as though this book would remain in its pristine and untouched state.

The warmth of the beautiful sunshine that was now draping their fields brought with it an endless list of chores that needed to be completed. The garden had to be tilled and planted, as did the crop fields. Their small assortment of livestock had been blessed with offspring; these had to be tended to. Their cow needed to be milked, clothes mended, ditches dug, trees cleared, and a thousand other things, all before breakfast.

The list of chores was longer, it seemed to James, than there was enough time in the day to complete them. Yet somehow, by the time the sun set each evening, the family had managed to complete that day's work. They would then eat supper and retire, exhausted, into their beds.

At the end of such an evening during the second week of June, James' older brother Jean brought up the topic of the book that they had been given. The family was seated around the old wobbly table where they ate supper. Marguerite had just placed their meal of cabbage soup on the table and sat down to join her family.

"That is, err, delicious looking, my dear," offered Papa. "James, could you grab one of the fish that you brought home yesterday and throw it on the fire?"

Marguerite looked deeply offended.

"My dear, your boiled cabbage is wonderful!" Papa ate a large bite. "I just don't want James to think that we don't like his fish," Papa looked at James and winked. This seemed to placate

Marguerite.

As they waited for the fish to finish cooking, Jean looked up at Papa. "Papa," he began in a measured tone. "I read the book that Barthélémy left us."

James was momentarily stunned. Causing him to choke on his cabbage, losing some of it down the front of his shirt.

"Disgusting, James!" cried Marguerite. "If you are going to eat like a cow, then go downstairs!"

James considered making a remark back to Marguerite about how she looked like a cow, but decided that he appreciated his life too much to do anything so foolish. Instead, James waited until Marguerite was looking in the other direction, away from the table. James then glanced over at Daniel and mooed quietly, while purposely letting more cabbage fall down his face. They both burst into laughter. By the time Marguerite turned back around, James had cleaned up the cabbage from off his face and shirt, and was sitting quietly with a completely innocent looking expression.

Teasing Marguerite aside, James wondered how Jean had found time to read. He barely had enough time between chores to eat and sleep, let alone to participate in a leisurely activity like reading. But as James thought about it, he supposed that it was only a matter of time before Jean would have read it. Yes, of course he must have read the book. There wasn't a book or sheet of paper, for that matter, within ten miles that Jean had not read. James imagined that it would have been too much of a temptation for Jean to have seen it there day after day, looking so new, just begging to be read. At some point Jean was bound to be overcome by curiosity. Even if it meant not sleeping at night.

"Read it, did you?" Papa chuckled. "I thought you might. Tell us then, son, what did you think?"

Jean paused, not sure how to proceed. Finally, he offered a confident, albeit subdued bit of counsel. "I think that you also need to read it, Papa."

Over the next few weeks Papa took Jean's advice. Each evening, as the family lay down for the night, Papa sat down in his old wooden chair, and passed the remaining hours of the evening reading. Occasionally Papa would stretch as he read, but he did not say anything about the contents of the book. James watched Papa for clues as to how he was receiving what Barthélémy had claimed was a book of new scriptures. He appeared to be at least somewhat interested in the book. Papa did not look overly sleepy, or as though he were only reading the book in order to please Jean.

But James could not be certain. Perhaps he was just pretending to read. Or more likely, reading the words with his eyes, while really thinking about the business of the farm. Papa was very good at making his children feel valued. If Jean had asked him to read a book detailing the day to day life of the common ant, or some other equally dreadful subject, James was sure that Papa would have obliged him. If for no other reason than to show respect for his son.

By late June, the tilling and planting were completed. The family's energy then began to focus on the endless job of keeping weeds out of their garden and crop fields. They rose with the sun, completed the regular chores, taking care of the livestock, gathering eggs, mending clothing, and taking care of repairs. Then, after breakfast, they would all gather to spend the rest of the day on their hands and knees, crawling on the ground, pulling out these offending and unwanted plants. It was tedious, dirty, and often painful work.

Today was no different. As the family worked to remove these noxious greens from their small southern crop field, James' back began to ache, as it often did during the long days that they spent weeding. In an effort to relieve this pain, James arched his back downward. He could not stand up, nor could he stop working. If he did, Papa would remind him that there was too much work to get done, and there wasn't time for anyone to be idle. As he flexed his back muscles, James turned his head sideways, catching a glimpse of Barthélémy Pons and his family approaching in the distance.

James thought about informing the rest of his family about who was on their way to greet them, but Marguerite beat him to it. The sound of the Pons family's voices began to carry across the field on the wind, toward James and his family.

Hearing their voices, Marguerite squealed with excitement.

"Papa, look!" she cried. "May I go and welcome Lydia and Marie, Papa?!" she implored.

"I suppose now is as good a time as any to take a *short* break," answered Papa, putting emphasis on the word 'short.' "I have some business I need to discuss with Barthélémy anyway."

Papa wiped his forearm across his brow, and carefully stood up. "Let's go greet our guests," he encouraged.

As the family returned to the house, their visitors were waiting for them just outside the front door. "Afternoon, Jean," called Barthélémy.

"Good afternoon, Barthélémy!" smiled Papa. "I am glad you stopped by. I have something I need to discuss with you. Ah, but first, tell me what has brought you here? And on a work day, no less!"

"We are on our way to a baptism. New converts are joining our church. Your farm is on the way, so we thought that we would stop by and invite you to come along."

Papa thoughtfully responded, "Barthélémy, I have read the book you left us, and I have some questions to ask you. A baptism? Yes, I think we will go and see that!"

With that, they abandoned their afternoon chores, and made their way across the valley with the Pons family. James couldn't remember a time when Papa had allowed them to simply walk away from chores. Papa had always been absolutely firm when it came to getting your chores done. "If we do not complete our labors, then we will not eat, and if we do not eat, then we will die." James had heard these words so many times that they had become a part of his own core beliefs. And now, here they were, on a day that was not the Sabbath, just walking away from a field that desperately needed weeding, so they could go and see yet another innocent Waldensian leave their faith behind, as they were led into the darkness that was the Mormon Church.

As the group walked down to the Pellice River where the service was to take place, the narrowness of the trail forced them to walk either single file or occasionally in twos, side by side. Lost in thought, James ended up alone at the back of the group. Immediately in front of him were Marguerite and Marie, and in front of them, Jean and Lydia were walking side by side.

James could not hear anything that either Jean or Lydia were saying to each other. The loud and silly laughter of Marguerite would have drowned out the sound of a donkey giving birth. Whatever it was they were discussing, they both appeared to James to be greatly interested in the topic.

Jean and Lydia were not overly loud or boisterous, as were Marguerite and Marie. Instead, they simply smiled at one another, and carried on a conversation the entire trip from their family farm all the way to the banks of the Pellice River. Their discussion must have been very interesting. James could not remember a time when Jean had ever spoken for such an extended period of time to anyone.

The baptismal service was a quaint affair. A very small

group of ragged and impoverished farmers, none of them trained in seminary, or possessed of any special talents that would make them stand out in the world, all huddled together underneath the mountain pines. Basked in the alpine sunshine, they began the meeting with a short prayer. This prayer was rather different than anything James had ever heard before. The first thing that made this prayer seem peculiar was that it was not offered by a pastor. Instead, the voice of the prayer had been a lay member of the congregation. Odder still was the fact that this person had not read the prayer or, for that matter, even prepared it ahead of time. Instead, he spoke simply as though he were carrying on a conversation directly with God.

After the prayer, a man who introduced himself as Daniel Justet began to speak. He talked about how he had been baptized in this very same river a year earlier. He explained that at the time his wife and children had not joined him in his conversion to Mormonism.

When the missionaries had first visited them, Mr. Justet described how he had been convinced of the truthfulness of their message right away, but his wife had remained skeptical. She had been discouraged by the barbes, and also by her parents, in following her husband's example. But now, a little more than a year later, and after many months of prayer and study, she was now finally ready to accept the covenant of baptism. Along with their three children.

After he concluded his comments, the family then made their way down to the river bank. What happened next was even more surprising and unexpected than had been the bizarre prayer. Mr. Justet entered the river, and taking each by the hand, he baptized his own wife and children! James was astonished. He thought that only pastors could administer in the sacred sacraments of the gospel. And yet, here stood not a pastor, but a simple farmer, baptizing his own family. Truly these Mormons are odd, James thought to himself.

After the service concluded, James and his family returned to their farm, once again walking alongside the Ponses.

"Tell me, Barthélémy," inquired Papa "was that man a priest? He said he had only been a member of your church for a year."

"Indeed he is a priest," smiled Barthélémy. "But then, so are all the men in our church."

"All the men are priests?" Papa remarked. "But then, who

leads your services?"

"We take turns," answered Barthélémy. "One of us is called to serve as the leader of the group for a time, and then he is released and another is called to take his place. Our first leader here in the valleys was Lorenzo Snow. When he left us for Switzerland, Jabez Woodard took his place. Eventually someone else will be called to serve in Jabez's stead."

"But any of these . . . err . . . priests can officiate in your sacraments?" Papa inquired.

"Yes, indeed. Any man, if he is worthy, can administer the sacraments of baptism and the holy supper."

Over the next few days, Papa and Jean spoke frequently of the book, the baptismal service, and the Mormon sect that was slowly gathering converts in the valleys, until in early July, when the unthinkable happened. Sunday had arrived as usual, and the family was preparing to go to temple. As the girls finished brushing out their hair, Papa entered the main upstairs room of the house and announced that the family would not be going to temple that day, but would instead be attending the Mormon services.

"Papa!" cried Marguerite. "No! I promised my dear friend Lousia that I would sit next to her this week during temple."

"Marguerite, my darling, I am sure that Lousia will forgive you. And anyway, aren't you the least bit curious what these Mormon services are like?"

"Curious about their services?!" laughed Marguerite. "Why would I care about the services of a tiny group of strange people that no one takes seriously?"

"What about your friends Lydia and Marie?" countered Papa. "Are they strange?"

Marguerite had been ready for this, and had her reply out almost before Papa had finished speaking, "Papa, she smiled. Lydia and Marie don't have any choice. Their Papa makes them go."

This, however, did not have the affect that Marguerite had anticipated. Papa simply smiled and replied, "It sounds like they have a very wise Papa. Now finish getting ready!"

Backed into a corner by her own logic, and not knowing what else to say, Marguerite pouted and walked outside to await the rest of the family. By and by, each emerged from their home and took a seat outside, awaiting the Ponses, who were to lead the way to the Cardon farm.

The moment that they arrived, Jean eagerly walked over to

Lydia, while pointing to a page in the Book of Mormon, and asked, "Lydia, have you read these verses here about this Amulek?"

Lydia smiled and answered, "He is the man who received the prophet Alma into his home, is he not?"

"Indeed he is," smiled Jean, holding Lydia's gaze briefly then continuing. "He lived in a place where no one believed in the words of this Alma fellow. All his kin and all his friends thought he was a heretic. But he knew that Alma was a prophet. And so he stood by him anyway."

"I wonder," paused Jean.

"Go on," encouraged Lydia.

"Well, it just strikes me that you are in a very similar situation, are you not?" asked Jean.

Lydia remained quiet as the two of them began to walk side by side down the trail. This time, James made sure that he stayed close enough to them to overhear what they were discussing.

Jean continued, "You and your family, you have found something that you believe to be true. Everyone around you thinks that you have been deceived. Even your own family, your closest friends, they all have turned you away, and will no longer talk to you. And yet you persevere in your faith."

Jean paused and looked into Lydia's eyes. "Lydia, I think you are amazing. I mean to say," he paused awkwardly, "what I meant was that your family is amazing," he concluded, blushing.

Lydia smiled and replied, "When you know something is true, Jean, you have to follow it, no matter where that path may lead you."

Yuck! Thought James. This was not the intelligent conversation he had expected. He slowed his pace so that he was soon once again at the back of the group, where he could be left alone with his own thoughts.

As the group continued toward the home of Philippe Cardon where the services were to be held, James pondered the strangeness of the day. Papa had taught him on many occasions that during the warm season, one should never miss temple unless they were dying. Even then, they should crawl to temple if they could. And yet today, the six of them, all healthy, were not only skipping temple, but even worse, they were traveling to the home of a heretical stranger to attend a secret meeting that was completely outside of the authority of the barbes. He was both frightened by the prospect of going against the counsel of the barbes, and also like Papa, rather curious to find out what this meeting would be like.

Running to catch up with Papa he asked, "Papa, why do the err . . . Mormons meet in a home instead of a temple?"

"When the missionaries first arrived in the valleys, the barbes allowed them to preach in the temples for a short time. You remember when they visited our temple?"

"You mean, when they claimed there was a new prophet, and more scriptures?!" smirked Marguerite loudly enough that the Pons family could hear her.

"Yes . . . , well, they have since been banned from temple," continued Papa.

"I should hope so!" offered Marguerite, who was still sulking from having to miss her appointment with her friend Louisa.

James knew that the barbes had preached against listening to the Mormons. He supposed that it made sense that they would also not allow them to preach in the temples.

"Papa, why do the barbes say that the Mormons are, um, evil?" James asked quietly so that he would not offend their traveling companions.

"Because, my boy, these Mormon missionaries began to be successful. They began to have converts."

"Converts, Papa?" asked James inquisitively.

"Yes, son. Some of the people believed them," said Papa.

"Some people will believe anything," replied Marguerite, more to herself than to the rest of the group.

Having spent a lot of time with Jabez Woodard and with the Pons family, James had learned to like them a great deal. True, they believed differently than his family did, but they were good people, and James trusted them. They didn't strike him as deceptive, much less as fools, as Marguerite had labeled them. James wondered what his Papa thought of them. Papa had read their book. He had then taken the family to one of their baptismal services, and was now taking them all to a Sunday service. James wondered why Papa would do these things. Was he just curious about their new friends, or was it something more? Could Papa be . . . converting, as he had called it? Did he believe the missionaries?

And then, what about Jean, his older brother? James

remembered that it had been Jean who had told Papa that he needed to read the Mormon book. Now that James thought about it, Jean did seem especially delighted today to be going to the Mormon meeting. Could it be that Jean, who James considered to be the most intelligent of his siblings, was also converting?

These thoughts were very difficult for James' young mind to process. What did all of this mean for him? During his thirteen years he had often been taught that the Waldensian people had the light of the gospel and that it was they who had carried it, when all around them the world and fallen into apostasy. He had been so proud of the role that his people had played in the Lord's plan. In the way that they had maintained that light, despite monumental opposition, all the way up until the time the great reformers also found the gospel light, and then worked to spread it throughout the rest of Europe.

And now, what was he supposed to believe about his beloved mountain faith? Had they also apostatized somewhere along the way? Perhaps not as fully as Rome, but somehow, had they also lost the purity of their doctrines And if that was the case, then had all their struggling and suffering to preserve these teachings been in vain? After all, what was the point of preserving something if it too was incorrect?

James felt his world turning upside down. Doubts began to form in his mind about his once unquestioned faith. For the first time in his life he was unsure about who he was and what he believed.

"Papa?" he said, in a tone that sounded more nervous than he had intended.

"Yes, my boy?"

"Do you believe them?"

Papa stopped walking. He bent down so that he could look directly into James' eyes. Grabbing him by his waist, he gently replied, "Yes, my boy."

1853

Chapter Ten

Words of a Prophet

The Cardon family home was too small to accommodate the growing Mormon congregation, a group whose numbers today had swelled by six more curious investigators.

Fortunately, the day's alluringly mild weather allowed the assemblage of alpine worshipers to meet outside. There, with the jagged mountains as a backdrop, Jabez Woodard opened the service by welcoming their guests.

"Brothers and sisters, before we begin our meeting, we have a new family among us that I would like to acquaint you all with."

James was amused by the seemingly informal nature of the meeting. It was unlike any church meeting he had ever attended before. Where the barbes employed ritual, order, and tradition, these Mormons seemed to prefer friendship, open discussion, and mutual edification. To James, it almost felt more like a temple picnic than a rigid temple meeting. James liked this informality, although he was not certain that it was entirely appropriate for a Sunday service.

Jabez continued the meeting by next introducing each member of the group to James' family. One by one, Jabez asked each member of the congregation to stand from off the grassy hill, or the stump, or the mossy rock that they occupied. Once standing, he then invited them to share how they had come to be a part of this group.

James was fascinated by the many different conversion stories. Papa had been right. Those missionaries who had visited their temple so long ago had indeed had success in finding converts. Perhaps not in terms of the number of converts that they had found; the group itself being smaller than a modest clutch of spring chickens. But the smallness of the group was overshadowed by the strength and fervency of the conviction that filled their hearts. It appeared to James that these young Mormon hatchlings believed their doctrine with all of their souls.

As James listened to their stories, an unfamiliar emotion began to creep into his heart. It was a tranquil sort of peace that he had never felt before. It was not loud or overwhelming enough to drown out other emotions, but it was definitely there. Something that spoke to him of the sacredness of what he was hearing. Surely during one of the many temple sermons that James had attended, a barba must have spoken of this serene feeling, though he could not find any memories of such a topic ever being discussed in his mind.

Now that he thought about it, the barbes hadn't ever really spoken of any type of feelings at all. They had, however, spoken often on the subject of light. Indeed, they had taught him that the Waldensians were the light of the world. James supposed that this must be what he was feeling. It must be light, as though a new flame were growing inside of him.

James had always enjoyed temple. The rituals had a dependable sameness to them. It was during these temple sermons that he believed that he was closest to heaven.

But now, here among the Mormons, something bothered him. James wondered why he had never felt this– this light during a temple meeting. Why hadn't it been until he sat on a grassy hill next to the Cardon family farm that these warm feelings had found their way into his heart?

The last family to introduce themselves were their hosts. Philipe and Marie Cardon had six children, four sons and two daughters. The Cardons had joined the Church eighteen months earlier in the middle of winter. Philipe shared how one by one, they each had stepped into the icy waters of the Angrogna river to be baptized.

Winter in the Alps was brutal enough, James thought to himself. Why would anyone want to swim in a river?

"We knew that it would be cold, but we were too anxious to wait for warmer weather. Once we had heard that the authority to officiate in the ordinance of true baptism had been restored, we determined to avail ourselves of it straight away!"

Philipe's voice began to crack, "But as each of us stepped down into the river, you will not believe me when I tell you, but the river was not cold. Although there was ice everywhere in the river, the water immediately around each of us felt warm."

The quiet feeling that had been occupying James' heart gathered additional strength as he listened to Philipe. Each of the

Cardon children confirmed the words of their Papa; that they too had felt only warm water on that cold day. To James, this seemed to be a miracle! He was not sure how he felt about miracles. He thought they no longer occurred. Hadn't they all ended with the death of the Apostles?

After these individual testimonies, Jabez Woodard then began his sermon. He taught of a young American boy about the same age as James, who asked God to tell him which church was true.

James was fascinated by this tale. This was one of the doctrines that the barbes had warned the people to be wary of. They had taught them that the Mormons believed in false prophets. James had expected this false prophet to be a grown man, not a boy like himself. How could a fourteen year old boy lead so many astray? James was himself just a few weeks away from his fourteenth birthday. If James had told his family and friends that he had received a message from God, they would not have believed him. They would have immediately seen through his ruse. Being the youngest in the family, he had a hard time convincing them that he could bathe himself properly, let alone become their spiritual leader.

Unless God had really visited him, then perhaps the Lord would make his family believe him. But that was not likely. The barbes had made it clear that God no longer called prophets in our day. Still, James imagined what it would be like as a boy his age to be used by God to do something so important. The barbes spent years preparing for their callings. They had to go to seminary, and pass difficult examinations. Yet, here was Jabez claiming that a fourteen year old, with no training of any kind, had been appointed by God to the most important position on Earth, that of a prophet. It was a fantastic tale, even if it wasn't true. A boy prophet, like Samuel of old. If he were a boy prophet, then everyone would have to listen to him. He could tell them what to do, while he tended to more spiritual matters, like reading and studying. James smiled to himself.

After the meeting, James and his family remained with the Cardons for much of the afternoon. Papa spent the time asking a variety of questions about the Mormon Church, while James sat quietly listening.

Marguerite, who had no interest in hearing anything more about the Mormons, employed her afternoon toward adding the two Cardon daughters, Marie and Catherine, to her collection of ardent admirers. Including Marie Pons, the four of them huddled together a short distance away from the rest of the group, sitting playfully in the grass. Marguerite acted as their leader, while the other three vied for her approval and attention. Their laughter occasionally being carried through the air toward James. To James, their levity seemed oddly inappropriate. True, the services themselves were now concluded, but to James, something still lingered. The light he had felt earlier still remained in his heart. To James, this little hillside seemed to be a special place now. He could not understand how these four silly girls could behave in such an irreverent manner while standing on such sacred ground. Unless of course, to them the ground wasn't sacred at all. James reminded himself that it was, after all, just a crop field. Although he couldn't explain why, to him, this hill was now something more. It was the place where for the first time in his life he had felt that special feeling of light.

ဢ

It had been a remarkable and beautiful Sabbath service. Jean felt that it was an honor and a privilege to have been invited.

He enjoyed the stories shared by each of the congregants, as well as the sermon which had been preached by Jabez. Equally enjoyable, thought Jean, was the company. Lydia Pons was different than anyone he had ever met before.

Surviving in the mountains left little time for courting girls. Marriages were often made out of convenience rather than love. When one spends all their time on their own farm, with the exception of the Sabbath, the only members of the opposite sex that one meets are those who live very close by.

Jean knew all the local girls as well as he knew his own sisters. And what was worse was that they all felt like sisters to him. There were only four or five that were close enough in age to him to be potential mates. He had grown up with them in temple. Each of them had visited their family farm on a number of occasions over the years to call on his sisters.

Not Lydia Pons. She was a novelty. Her family lived far enough away that Jean had never laid eyes on her until that day a few weeks earlier when her father had stopped by to introduce their family.

Jean was not so foolish as to suppose himself in love with Lydia. He was certain that he would have been as equally impressed by any of the local girls if, like Lydia, they had suddenly appeared in his life for the first time.

For Jean, it was refreshing to talk to someone new. Someone whom he didn't already know so well that they couldn't surprise him. Jean supposed that this too was a part of what interested him in Lydia, the fact that she could surprise him. What secrets did she hold within her? The other girls in the area certainly could not surprise him. Jean knew them so well that he could predict their reactions to virtually any set of circumstances. But not Lydia Pons. Who knew how she might react? It was a complete mystery. A mystery that Jean felt was worth exploring. How did people from around the valleys react to things? How did they talk? How did they think? He wasn't courting her, he was just studying; learning more about others who lived farther away.

She was beautiful, though. Especially when she smiled. Her lips curling back, revealing her teeth. Her brown eyes glistening when she made eye contact with him. Making her smile was a reward worth working for. There was nothing wrong with enjoying her beauty, Jean thought to himself. He was just being friendly.

Good looks and curious behavior were not the only things

that set Lydia Pons apart. Above all, it was her intelligence that endeared her to Jean as someone worth keeping company with. Waldensian girls didn't attend subsidiary as the boys did. There were a few schools for girls in the valleys, but most young Waldensian ladies were taught at home. They were still expected to learn to read and to memorize the scriptures, but they had to learn these skills from their fathers or brothers. The barbes had very limited resources. It was not that they did not value the educational prospects of girls, but rather, they had to prioritize how to accomplish the mission of educating everyone. If the males were educated, then someone in the home was sure to have the skills to teach everyone else, thereby insuring that all would be edified.

In theory, it was a sound policy. But it did not always work as effectively as the barbes hoped. Most girls did learn to read, but usually not as well as their brothers. After all, it is difficult to learn to read better than those who are teaching you.

Lydia was not only an excellent reader, but had put this talent to good use. She seemed as well read to Jean as he was, perhaps even more so. Lydia had read many of his favorite books, something that none of the local girls had done. However, Jean found that she interpreted these books quite differently than he himself did.

Jean saw the stories that he read through the eyes of a son and future father, trying to survive and protect his family, such was the case with the adventures of King Arthur. To Jean, this had always been a story about the powerful King Arthur, protecting the rights and freedoms of those who were weaker than himself. Lydia didn't see it that way at all. For her, it was a romantic tragedy about a woman who was trapped between her duty and her heart. Jean could see her point, although he didn't think that was what the tale itself had been about. When Jean had tried to convince Lydia that she was misreading the plot and giving too much emphasis to a minor part of the book, he was delighted to see that she did not back down. She held her ground and pushed back, telling Jean that he was too much of a man to see beyond the outer shell and that he was missing the underlying themes. It was wonderful to debate with someone who had enough intelligence and knowledge to make a reasonable argument, even if she was wrong and too stubborn to admit it.

Today, Jean's mind was on the Book of Mormon, especially given the sermon that Jabez had just concluded, where he taught that these scriptures were translated by a young boy prophet. Of particular interest to Jean was the notion that this Joseph Smith had been given all of these revelations in response to a simple prayer that he had offered.

As Jean and Lydia walked together toward the Cardon's small barn where the rest of the group was sitting, Jean turned to Lydia and asked her the question that was on his mind.

"Lydia, does God really answer prayers in such a direct manner as Jabez taught today? He wouldn't really make a personal visit to a young boy, would he?"

"Why wouldn't he?" she replied.

"If he does, then why hasn't he visited every fourteen year old boy who has ever asked for advice?"

"Are you envious, Jean? Are your feelings hurt because God did not visit you?" Lydia teased, smiling.

"Not envious," replied Jean, "dubious."

"You have to ask. Joseph Smith did not get his answer until he asked the Lord for guidance."

"I have asked for many things in prayer, and I have never had any heavenly manifestations," retorted Jean.

"What did you ask for?" inquired Lydia patiently.

"I don't know, for safety, for a bountiful crop, for good weather, for relief from the blight."

"Ah, so you did not ask anything that requires an answer then, did you?" she smiled.

Jean thought for a moment before replying, "Those all require answers."

"Do they?" she asked. "Then tell me, Jean, exactly what answer does the Lord need to give you when you pray for a bountiful crop?"

Jean was beginning to see her point, but did not like having to admit that he had been wrong. He did his best to come up with an answer that would avoid his having to do so. "He should confirm that he heard me, and that he is on the job," he offered lamely.

"Oh yes, Jean, by all means, because the Lord is not busy at all with running the world. He should take the time to tell you that he heard your prayer. Why don't you try asking something important. Not just important to you, but also important to him. Something that will cause him to pause and take note. Something that will make him want to answer you."

Jean was impressed by Lydia's passion. But he couldn't

think of anything he could pray about that was so important that the Lord himself would actually pause and take notice. They had now reached a bench that was fixed alongside the Cardon barn. They sat down before continuing their conversation.

"You think I am crazy, don't you?" Lydia asked in mock offense. Then, in a voice that was unmistakably sincere, she continued, "Jean, you don't believe that there is something important enough in your life for the Lord himself to take notice." She placed her hand on top of his.

It was a wonderful sensation that caused his brain to go completely blank. Suddenly he was not intelligent at all. He was no better than a rock, completely incapable of independent thought.

She paused, looking directly into his eyes. "Jean, it's you," she smiled. "You are important enough to God that a question about yourself, about your own salvation, will cause the Lord to take a break from his labors in order to answer you."

Had she just called him important? Or was she saying that he was only important to God? Fortunately, she removed her hand from his, which allowed his mind to once again start working.

"You are suggesting that if I ask God a question about my

salvation, that he will personally come down and answer me?" Jean asked skeptically.

"Sort of, yes," she said, doubting that she was getting her point across. "He may not visit you, but yes, he will personally answer you."

"Not visit me personally? But I thought that was what we were talking about? How then is he going to answer me? By sending me a post?"

Lydia sighed quietly, and then shared something that Jean could tell was very personal to her. "Jean, what I am telling you, I know, because he answered me. No– " she held up her hand to stop Jean from interrupting, "he did not visit me, and no, he did not send me a post. He answered me in here," she said, placing her hand on her chest. "Jean, if you ask him, he will tell you in your heart."

"So I should ask him about my salvation?" Jean said, still doubting her, "and he will answer me in my heart? What should I ask then, 'am I saved?'"

"Ask him the question that is on your mind Jean. Ask him the question that you have been contemplating."

Jean had no idea what she meant by that. What question was on his mind? They had been talking about God visiting mankind. Did she want him to ask God if he indeed visited men? Not men generally, but more specifically, had he visited with this Joseph Smith?

That was an interesting question, thought Jean. If God really did visit with Joseph Smith, then he truly was a prophet. Suddenly this seemed to Jean to be a very important thing to find out. If Joseph Smith was a prophet, then he ought to be listening to the message that he had brought to the world.

According to Lydia, Jean could ask God questions that had to do with his own salvation, and if he did that, the Lord would pause long enough to answer him, not through a visit, but through a feeling in his heart.

Jean supposed that knowing whether or not a prophet were truly called of God qualified as important enough to relate to his own salvation. What could it hurt? No one had to know that he had prayed for such a thing. If he didn't get an answer, then no one would know that he had foolishly asked. It was not as though asking incurred any commitment on his part. It was the least he could do for his new friend Lydia. How could he be a good friend if he didn't take her counsel?

&

At last, James felt as though he were catching up to his older brothers. Throughout his entire life he had been too small, too weak, too short, or too inexperienced. He was not yet as tall as Jean, or as strong as Daniel, but he was now tall enough and strong enough to carry his share of the burdens that came with looking after a successful farm.

James no longer required constant supervision. Or more accurately, his siblings now accepted the fact that they did not need to always be nearby to boss him around. They trusted in his ability to do a good job on his own. Something he had known he could do for a long time, but that they were just now beginning to appreciate and accept.

It was a warm and beautiful morning. The sun was rising overhead, casting its orange and pink glow across the clouds. James began the morning by milking Marma, their dairy cow. She was old and didn't produce as much as she once had, despite having been recently refreshed, having bore a spring calf. But she was reliable enough to keep the family supplied with what they needed.

Before milking her, James settled her into her stall, just as he had been taught to do by Papa. He filled a bucket with grain from the field so that she would eat contentedly while he worked her udders. He then sat down at her side on a small stool and began the methodical and repetitive motions that would cause the white frothy milk to squirt out into the small wooden pail.

When Papa had first taught James how to milk Marma, he had been excited to learn the craft. James had quickly become disappointed, though, at how difficult the chore had turned out to be. It took a great deal of precision, and very strong hand muscles. James remembered how much his hands used to ache after milking her. But now, nearly three years later, the muscles in his hands had adapted, they no longer hurt or even got tired.

The first time he had milked Marma it had taken him nearly an hour to finish, only to then have her kick the bucket, splashing milk all over himself and the ground. He left, frustrated and angry. But he learned from the experience, and could now finish the job in ten minutes. He learned to anticipate Marma's movements, and to hobble her legs with a rope so that she could not kick. What had begun three years earlier as a very tiring and frustrating chore, was now a quick job that he could complete half asleep.

After milking her, James returned Marma to her pen where he then rewarded her with a flake of hay. James then hauled several pails full of water from a nearby stream to a trough so that Marma could drink.

He fed and watered their three sheep and their thirteen chickens. He gathered the five eggs that had been laid by some of the hens, and brought them into the house, giving them to Marguerite to use for their meals that day.

Going back outside, James then grabbed a shovel and returned to the corrals where he mucked out the pens and hauled the manure to the compost pile where it would be allowed to rot for a year before being added to the garden and crop fields.

James worked hard so that he would have his regular chores done before breakfast. This was the expectation that Papa had, and James did not want to disappoint him. At breakfast, Papa would have a list of chores that he would divide up between the members of the family. If his regular morning chores were not yet done, then they would get in the way of what Papa wanted the family to accomplish that day. He would hold up the progress of the entire family, and that was something James was not willing to allow happen. By working diligently, hard, and fast, James was able to finish his last morning chore, which was checking the hooves of their animals and clipping them as needed, just as Marguerite called everyone for breakfast.

"Daniel, today I need you to finish reaping the barley," Papa began, as they ate their bread.

"Yes, Papa," answered Daniel, "I should be able to finish today. I only have a small section of the barely field left."

"Excellent," smiled Papa.

"Marguerite, between meals, can you please clean the house?"

Marguerite began to answer before Papa had finished speaking. "Papa! That is not fair! Why do I have to clean the entire house by myself? Why can't someone help me?!" she pouted.

Closing his eyes, Papa took a deep breath before allowing himself to continue, "Please, just do the best that you can, my dear. I need the others to work outside."

James did not understand why Papa allowed Marguerite to get away with being so lazy. The only time he made her work outside was on days when they all weeded together. James would never get away with an attitude like hers. With so much work to be done before winter, they needed all the help they could get, and Marguerite would spend most of her day in the house cooking bad food and pretending to work.

"Antoinette, dear, what will you be working on today?" Papa asked. Papa usually did not assign Antoinette chores as he did everyone else. Since Mama's passing, Antoinette had stepped into the role of housekeeper. She knew better than Papa did what chores needed attending to. She had earned his and everyone else's trust.

"I have a couple shirts and pants to mend, and then I hope to finish spinning the wool we collected yesterday into yarn." Antoinette smiled gently as she softly answered Papa.

"Very good, my dear," Papa smiled back at her. "Jean, I want you to take James and cut down the six fig trees by the south fence that are nearly dead. Get them cut down, get the wood chopped, and stack it by the barn. Tomorrow you two can dig out the stumps."

"I will be weeding the garden, and then later working with Daniel to tie the barley stems into straw bundles," Papa concluded.

The family finished their breakfast, and then Jean and James walked together toward the shed where the saws and ropes were stored.

"James, we will need to first cut the branches off of each tree on the south side. This will make the south side lighter so that when we fell them, they will fall to the north. Otherwise they will smash the fence to bits, and we will have to rebuild that as well."

"You grab the rope, and I will bring the saws," Jean instructed.

From the shed, they walked through the tall mountain grass toward the southern fence that lined their little farm. The sun was now rising into view, causing the temperature to climb. James could already tell that it was going to be a hotter than normal, and uncomfortable day.

As Jean climbed into the first tree, James tried to anticipate what he would need. He grabbed one of the saws and handed it up to Jean. Without being asked, James then grabbed the other saw and climbed the tree just to the west of Jean. James watched Jean for clues about what to do next and copied him.

Jean began to saw off branches, and so James did likewise. It was hard work, but James found that he could keep up with his older brother. As he worked, his arms began to burn, screaming for a break. But James refused to give in to the pain unless Jean did. He was not going to be slower than Jean, no matter how much it hurt!

James watched as Jean tossed his branch down, being careful to miss the fence. James copied him.

As they worked, Jean attempted to try and make conversation, "Do you pray, James?"

It was an odd question. Jean knew that he prayed. He did so all the time in front of him, as a matter of fact.

"I prayed last night, Jean! Remember? When Papa asked me to bless our supper?"

"Yes, that is true," replied Jean. After a few more minutes of silent working, Jean asked his question in a new way, "Do you pray when you are alone?"

James could not figure out what Jean was getting at. Why did he want to talk about prayer?

"There wouldn't be anyone to hear me," James answered in

amusement. Why would he pray when he was alone? Prayers were uttered in groups, at meal times, or at temple services.

They spent the remainder of the day working mostly in silence. Jean only spoke when it was necessary in order to explain to James what he needed him to do. James had never cut down a tree before, but by observing his brother and anticipating what he was doing, James found that he could be very helpful.

By supper time, they had felled all six trees, and had cut the branches and trunks into firewood. After supper they would go back out and stack the chopped wood alongside the barn as Papa had requested.

℘

Jean was exhausted. It had been a long day. Cutting down the fig trees had proven to be a labor intensive project. It was made all the more tiring by his little brother James, who had refused to rest the entire day. The little guy really could work hard, Jean thought to himself. He wasn't about to be outworked by his younger brother, and so Jean had doubled up his efforts, working much harder than usual. Jean didn't think that he would be able to last another day with him digging out the stumps. He might just have to let James see him take a few breaks during the next day.

Jean wanted nothing more than to go to sleep. He hurt, from the soles of his feet, to the tips of his fingers. His muscles cried out in agony knowing that they would be abused the next day as well. But as Jean lay in bed awaiting the certitude of sleep to quickly overcome his conscious thoughts, Jean continued to think about the subject that had been on his mind all day. Would he really pray and ask God to tell him if Joseph Smith had been called as a prophet? Did he dare make such a request to the Almighty?

When he had been with Lydia, he had decided there could be no harm in asking. He had convinced himself that no one had to know. But once Lydia had left and had taken her calming reassurance with her, new doubts had begun to crop up in his mind. It was true that no one would need to know about his prayer, but God would know. And he might be offended! James had confirmed this fear earlier in the day when he had laughed at Jean for even thinking about such a foolish prayer. Prayers are spoken in public, not private. They are meant to be heard by groups and are not something one does alone.

What if God became upset with Jean for daring to question

his faith? The barbes would undoubtedly counsel him that such a prayer would be blasphemous.   As Jean considered this, he imagined Lydia's smiling face and warm brown eyes. She would ask him at their next meeting if he had prayed. How disappointed she would be if he had to confess to her that he had not. Jean decided that he would pray, if only to give him an affirmative response to Lydia's impending question.

Checking that his brothers were asleep, Jean silently rolled out of bed and knelt upon the floor. Feeling awkward and intimidated by the strangeness of this new experience, he nearly jumped up and got right back into bed. Taking a deep breath, he calmed himself, and moved forward, determined to complete the task.

"Dear God," he paused before continuing. I sound like I am writing him a letter. How does one speak to a being as powerful as God? "Lord, please forgive me for, err, bothering you. My friend Lydia told me to," Jean paused again. That won't do! I can't blame Lydia, that is not fair. "Lord, I want to know if Joseph Smith was a prophet. I want to know if what the Mormons say is true."

Jean stood up and carefully climbed back into bed. There,

he had done it. He had prayed. Now he could tell Lydia that he
had done as she had asked, and that he had received no answer. He
did not see any angels, nor did he feel any special feeling in his
heart.

As Jean considered how he would explain this to Lydia, he
had an unfortunate thought occur to him. He realized that he had
not followed Lydia's instructions after all. She had told him to ask
God a question that required an answer. His question had not
been phrased properly. In his prayer, Jean had said that he wanted
to know if Joseph Smith had been a prophet, but he had not
actually asked God if he was. Jean had merely made a statement:
"I want to know if Joseph Smith was a prophet." That is not a
question. Jean sighed. Knowing that Lydia would not accept this,
he decided that he had better ask again.

Once again, Jean carefully climbed over his sleeping
brothers and out of bed. He once again knelt down and began to
pray.

"Lord, was Joseph Smith a prophet?" Jean paused,
wondering what he should do next. Should he keep asking the
same question over and over? Should he quietly wait for God to
answer, or should he just go back to bed? Jean decided that he

would wait for an answer. If God was going to answer, Jean had to give him the opportunity to do so.

After a few silent moments, Jean continued his prayer, speaking more personally than he had before. "Father, I believe that you want me to know the truth. Lydia promised that you would answer me. Please, Father, please tell me so that I can know for myself. Was Joseph Smith your prophet?"

As Jean spoke these words, his heart felt as though it were melting. A feeling of peace overtook him. A calm reassurance that was undeniable in the moment it was being felt. He might doubt it later, but right now, as he was feeling it, he knew with a strange absoluteness that Joseph Smith was indeed an actual prophet.

But what touched Jean more than this was that God had actually answered him. Him! He was no one of importance. And yet the God of Heaven and Earth had, as Lydia had promised, paused long enough to take note of his prayer, and had given him an answer! To Jean, it meant that God loved him, and this love was more precious than anything Jean had ever felt. Knowing that he was loved by the Lord caused Jean to roll over onto his side and quietly sob into the floor boards.

1853

Chapter Eleven

The Conflict of Conversion

The following Sunday, the family once again attended the Mormon services. As they arrived, the apprehension that had been present the week before, which had been caused by the unknown and by the unfamiliar, was gone. In its place, James felt a desire to really pay attention to the service. Now that he knew what to expect and didn't have to worry about what might happen, he was free to try and learn as much as he could about the message that the Mormons preached.

It wasn't that he believed what they were teaching, so much as that he wanted to understand it. He wanted to know why these . . . what was it Papa had called them? . . . these converts were so adamant in their beliefs. And, at the same time, why was their rejection of the precious mountain gospel so complete? How could they so resoundingly turn their backs on a gospel that their fathers had loved since the days of Christ? What was it about the Mormon message that caused faithful men and women to step out of and away from the traditions that had been cherished by their families for generations?

Now that his nerves were not on edge wondering what might happen, he could also try to ascertain what it was about the Mormons that made the barbes so upset. Why did they preach that the Mormons were a sect spawned by Satan? Why were they so afraid of a people that, to James, seemed to be kind, spiritual, and who appeared to represent everything that a Christian ought to stand for? What secrets had James missed? What dark side had he not seen during the last week's services? Papa believed the Mormons to be good people. He had even gone so far as to confess to James that he believed their message.

It was very difficult for James to have his entire world at odds with itself. He loved and respected both Papa and the barbes. His entire life they had always agreed with each other. Papa had taught James to respect and listen to the teachings that the righteous barbes shared. Until now, he had never had to choose between them. Life had been simple. Honoring Papa meant listening to the barbes. Listening to the barbes meant honoring Papa. The barbes taught to respect his Papa, while Papa had always instructed him to diligently follow the barbes.

Now, for the first time, Papa and the barbes did not agree with each other. And that disagreement was not over a small matter. Had they disagreed about whether fig pudding was delicious or not, James could have written the disagreement off as unimportant. But it was not a small matter that divided them. Indeed, the matter could not be more weighty. Their disagreement was over God and religion. If Papa was right, then not only were the barbes wrong, but they had always been so. If the barbes were right, then his Papa was apostatizing from his faith.

James was determined that today, as he sat in the Mormon service, he would be more observant. Today he would learn which of his mentors was right. The barbes, who thought the Mormons to be evil, or his Papa, who believed them to be good. He would not go to bed that night until he had come to terms with this inner conflict.

The meeting was once again held at the farm of the Cardon Family.

"Look, my boy," commented Papa, as they walked together toward the small group of Mormons standing just outside the Cardon home. "You see how there are no weeds in the vegetable garden? What does that tell you, James? And look over there! See how straight and well kept the fence is!"

James knew the answer that Papa was looking for. These types of questions were a common theme from Papa. He often pointed things like this out to James and his brothers. "It means that they are hard workers, Papa," answered James.

"That is right, my boy!" Papa firmly patted James on the back. "Hard work is the sign of a righteous man, James."

Usually Papa said something like, "hard work insures survival," or "only through hard work can we have nice things." "Hard work is the sign of a righteous man," was a new one that James had never heard Papa say before. The newness of the remark made it stand out. Instead of blending into a thousand other similar comments that had been made throughout James' young life, it gave him cause to stop and think.

What did Papa mean that having a garden free from weeds,

or a fence that stood in good repair was a sign of a righteous man? Why would he say that? Clearly Papa thought that the Cardon's papa was a righteous man, but did James agree? Could the missing garden weeds convince James that the Mormons were God's true followers? No, that might reassure Papa, but James thought to himself that he would need stronger evidence.

"Jean, what a pleasure to have you here again," smiled Jabez Woodard as he shook Papa's hand. "Please, come and join us!"

As he and his family walked the last few steps toward the others who had already arrived, they were greeted with many handshakes and warm smiles. To James, it felt like they were being treated as relatives who hadn't been seen in years, rather than recent acquaintances who had been absent only a week. Everyone was welcoming and genuinely glad that they had returned to another service.

James wondered if people usually did not return to their meetings the second time. Perhaps they were so excited to see them because people usually never came back.

Once again, their service was led by their friend Jabez. The meeting was the same as it had been the prior week, except that the message was different. Instead of preaching about the boy prophet,

Jabez instead talked about the Book of Mormon. James was, of course, already familiar with the book. They had a copy of their own in their home which both Jean and Papa had already read. But James had not read it. And as Jabez spoke, he realized just how little he himself knew about this book.

Jabez explained how God had led a group of ancient Israelites out of Jerusalem to the Americas. And how God had called prophets among this group of people, just as he had among their brethren in the old world. As Jabez preached, James again felt the precious feeling of light enter his heart. It was subtle, but it was there, making James feel as though everything was well in the world.

James had been so interested in the story of the Book of Mormon that he had completely forgotten about his self-assigned quest to determine who was right between Papa and the barbes. It wasn't until the meeting was over that James remembered he was supposed to be weighing the Mormon teachings against those of the barbes. He was supposed to be questioning their assertions. Instead, James had allowed himself to be lulled into a stupor and to be entertained by the stories that Jabez had told the group. Stories of a young adventurer named Nephi, and how he had cut the head off of a Jewish leader, wrestled a full-grown man to the ground, and used the power of God to shock his older brothers. James had been too busy thinking about how he would like to shock his brothers, to remember to find fault with the Mormons. Frustrated with himself at the missed opportunity, James returned home as confused as when he had started out that morning.

Later that evening, as the family prepared to eat their supper, James heard a knock on the door.

"James, my boy, go see who is at the door," Papa encouraged.

James promptly made his way downstairs, passing the animal pens as he walked to the front door. The old wooden door opened with little effort, revealing James' favorite mentor, Barba Peyrot, standing outside.

"James!" Barba Peyrot grabbed James' hand and shook it vigorously. "Is everything alright, young man?" he continued. "Is someone sick? We haven't seen you at temple for two weeks!"

Barba Peyrot did not wait to be invited in. He promptly pushed passed James, moving into the dimly lit lower room. James tried to explain that everyone was well enough off, and that they had skipped temple on purpose. But he couldn't seem to find the right words to express such a reprehensible thing to a barba.

"Yes, we err . . . we don't go to temple anymore . . . because . . . we like another church better . . . ?" No, that wouldn't do. Unable to think of anything to say, James simply stood there in silence.

Barba Peyrot took this silence, and the look of sheer panic on James' face as a validation of his concerns, that something was indeed terribly wrong with the family. Not waiting for any further explanation from James, Barba Peyrot headed upstairs to the main family living area.

"Jean! What a relief! From the expression on your boy's face, I thought for sure something tragic had happened. But you are all here and healthy enough. Tell me what then has kept you from temple these last two weeks?"

Without being invited to do so, Barba Peyrot took a seat on one of the few wooden chairs in the room. He looked up at Papa, anxiously awaiting a reply.

"Barba," began Papa. "Thank you for checking in on us. We are fortunate to have such kind friends in the Church."

James watched anxiously. How would Papa explain their

absence? And how would Barba Peyrot react to his explanation?

"These last two Sundays we attended services . . . with a different group of faithful believers."

"You went to a another temple, Jean? But why? The next closest temple is an awful lot farther to walk. And at your age! Did you have family to tend there?" Barba Peyrot was genuinely concerned about the family, which made it all the more difficult for James, who was beginning to feel guilty for having betrayed his favorite teacher.

"Not a different temple. We attended a service outside. A Mormon service, actually," Papa answered.

Although the Mormons were a small group, they had created an incommensurately large stir among the barbes. "Jean! Mormons? Why would you attend with those . . . with the likes of them?"

Papa answered with a firmness that surprised James. Like the testimonies which had been shared the prior week during the Mormon services that had carried such authority. "Because, Barba Peyrot, what they teach is true."

"True? Jean? How can you say such a thing? You do know

that they teach of a boy prophet in the Americas, don't you? And for heaven's sake, you know that they speak blasphemy about there being more scriptures?" Barba Peyrot was devastated by the prospect that one of his favorite families might have been infected by the devious Mormon plague.

"Yes, Barba, indeed, we have learned of all these things. We have come to know that through this American boy, God restored the fulness of his gospel. And once we learned this, the only real question left for us was would we listen to the voice of this young prophet, or ignore him? For my part, Barba, I believe that we have no choice but to follow him," Papa concluded.

Barba Peyrot was taken aback by the unexpected firmness of Papa's reply. As he spoke, his voice sounded deflated and genuinely saddened. "Jean, you of all people know that this cannot be true. We are God's chosen people. If a prophet were to be called, surely it would be from among one of us. From among the barbes! The notion that a boy with no religious training could be expected to do something so important, it's absurd!"

"I have always known the barbes to be good and righteous men. I have no idea why God works the way he does. But whether he calls a prophet here or in the Americas is not up to me.

All I can do is follow him, wherever he is," replied Papa.

Barba Peyrot glanced at James, despair dripping down his face. "And what about you James? Have you also abandoned your people? Have you also been lost to false beliefs and false prophets?"

The question struck James harder than as if he had been hit by a boulder bouncing down the mountainside. This was one of his most important friends. A mentor of great significance to him. How could James answer such an inquiry to someone that he looked up to? And in any event, James was still not certain how he felt. He was torn between the beliefs that his Papa now clearly accepted, and the faith that James had grown up with. James had always believed that his ancestors had played a special role in God's work, and that he was a son of this people chosen to preserve the gospel light and the scriptures. This certainty had given him his sense of purpose.

But the Mormons had something that his native faith didn't. Not just a living prophet or new scriptures, although James supposed that these things were also important. But there was something that James cherished more. Something that he had begun to grow dependent upon.

The Mormons carried with them that indescribable sacred feeling of light. A light that made James feel as though everything was right with the world, and that the Lord himself were somehow nearby. James only felt this way when he attended the Mormon services. When he was apart from them, he could not wait to return so he could once again get that feeling back.

Barba Peyrot continued looking at James expectantly. He was not going to let him get away without answering his question.

James glanced briefly over at Papa, who nodded, encouraging him to speak freely. Papa's eyes spoke comfort to James. He knew that Papa would not be angry if James' words indicated that he did not share Papa's beliefs about the Mormons. James was grateful that Papa was willing to let him make up his own mind.

Returning his attention to Barba Peyrot, James did his best to answer the question that still lay before him.

"I love our church, Barba Peyrot," James paused, trying to decide what he wanted to say next. "I have always been so proud of our people." This answer did not seem to satisfy Barba Peyrot, who still sat quietly, expecting James to say more. James could see that Barba Peyrot was going to force him to once and for all either accept or reject the Mormon teachings.

James was about to accept defeat and simply admit that he didn't know what he believed, but then something miraculous happened. Although he was not at a Mormon service, that cherished feeling of light began to fill James' heart. It seemed to give him courage, and also help him articulate words that he had not known were inside of him.

"But I believe the gospel is a puzzle," he looked anxiously at Papa, who smiled. "I think that the Lord chooses many different peoples, not just the Waldensians. And I believe . . ." James paused. His words became somewhat strained, as though he might cry. James thought that this was an odd way to feel. He was nearly fourteen years old after all. Why was he about to cry? And in front of his older brothers! He continued, "No, believe is not right. I know that what the Mormons teach is true." James finished.

His own answer astonished him. He had not set out to say that he knew the Mormon Church was true. How could he say such a thing? How could he know such a thing? Yet somehow he knew that he knew it. It was not just that he believed Papa, though he respected and trusted him. But somehow James knew independently of Papa that the message the Mormons had brought into their valleys was indeed true, though he had not known it until that very moment.

Barba Peyrot looked utterly stricken. To James, he seemed to be contemplating what to say next. How could he have lost this family to the Mormons? What could he do to bring them back?

James wanted to say that he was sorry. He wanted to tell his teacher that he would see him at temple next week, and that everything would be as it always had been. But he couldn't say any of these things, because they would not have been true. He would not see him at temple next week, because he would be going to the Mormon services. Papa was right. If God has called a prophet, then it does not matter whether he is Waldensian or American. Our only choice is whether we will follow him or not. In that moment, James knew that he had to follow the prophet, wherever it might lead him.

The silence was painful for James. He could see that he had severely wounded his old teacher. Thankfully, Papa's voice broke the quiet.

"Barba, we are still Waldensian. We have not betrayed our faith. We have added to it. Our people were indeed chosen to do a great work. And they did so. Now God has chosen an American people to further his work. This does not not take away from the mission that our people have played."

"Such nonsense, and from one of our best families!" Barba Peyrot replied, his voice now filled with unbearable disappointment. "False prophets, false scriptures, do all of you feel this way?" he asked the room at large.

"No," answered Marguerite, condescendingly. "We certainly do not all feel this way, Barba. Some of us feel rather differently."

"Well, Marguerite, that is very good to hear. Perhaps your beautiful spirit will reclaim the rest of your family," Barba Peyrot sighed. Marguerite blushed with pride.

1853

Chapter Twelve

Forward With Faith

Throughout the next few days, James revisited that Sunday's events in his mind over and over again. He worried about how his relationship with Barba Peyrot would now be altered, possibly forever.

James didn't look forward to returning to his final season of subsidiary. He wondered if Barba Peyrot would treat him with disdain, or worse, ignore him entirely.

Sensing this preoccupation, Antoinette inquired into what was bothering him one evening as they worked together shelling peas outside the family home. "Doing the right thing is not always easy, James," she counseled, "but it is still always the right thing to do."

"Right thing?" laughed Marguerite, who had been sitting in a nearby chair, pretending to help them work. "Yes, certainly Antoinette! Hurting a holy man who cares for you, and who made you one of his favorites, is the right thing to do! How could you say something so awful?"

Angered by Marguerite's abusive remarks toward Antoinette, Daniel, who had been standing a short distance away, took a couple of quick steps toward Marguerite. Realizing too late that she had gone too far, Marguerite recoiled, falling onto her back. Her momentum carried her sideways, causing her to roll over her chair and into the dirt. Daniel now towered above her, his massive form shaking as he spoke.

"You want to talk about saying awful things? What about what you said to Papa? Calling him foolish. Or what you said to Antoinette? Or James? Do you think that they have any choice? Can they just ignore God? Should they just sit passively by, wearing pretty things, while the Lord is calling them? All you care about is what people think of you!"

Daniel was about to continue his rebuke when he abruptly stopped, managing to gain control of his temper, and instead simply walked away. Marguerite pushed herself up off the ground. She brushed the dirt off her sore backside and promptly walked off in the opposite direction, looking as though she had been severely mistreated.

It had been a long time since Daniel had lost his temper. However, more surprising to James were the words that Daniel had spoken. These words made it appear as though perhaps Daniel was now also a believer. Like Papa, Jean and himself, Daniel too, it now seemed, had converted to Mormonism, and for that matter, James thought to himself, so had Antoinette. She had told him that it was not easy to do the right thing, but that he had done so. If she believed that his actions had been the right thing to do, then surely she must also have converted.

James took comfort in these thoughts. He looked up to his older siblings. The fact that all of them had converted helped to reinforce his own newly planted conversion. Well, all had converted except, of course, for Marguerite. And it was clear to James that she would likely never see things as the rest of the family did.

ร

On August 8, the entire family, except for Marguerite, was baptized by Jabez Woodard. It was an unseasonably hot summer day. Present in the congregation were most of the current converts as well as a few new investigators. Noticeably absent was Marguerite. She refused to support the family as they "turned their backs on the Waldensian people," as she had put it.

Papa had tried to get her to come and support them, but it was to no avail. Instead, Marguerite chose to spend her time with a group of local women and girls to whom she could gossip about the scandalous news of her family's actions that day.

After their baptism, Jabez explained that they would now also receive the gift of the Holy Ghost.

"What is the gift of the Holy Ghost?" asked James.

"The Holy Ghost is a member of the Godhead who testifies of truth," replied Jabez. "He makes us feel good inside."

"It's the Holy Ghost that makes me feel so good inside?" James inquired. At last he had a name for what he had been calling "light."

"Indeed, it is," answered Jabez. "And now you will have him with you all the time, young man! What do you think of that?"

James couldn't imagine having that feeling with him all the time. This blessing alone was worth all the hardships he had endured as a result of having converted to Mormonism.

"I think that it is wonderful," answered James sheepishly.

Jabez laughed, and rubbed his hand back and forth across the top of James' head.

℘

In time, the warmth of summer began to give way to another autumn. And although the weather began to cool, the burning of James' new faith remained warm within him.

In October, the chestnuts ripened, a final sign that winter was just weeks away. The family used these last few weeks of slightly tolerable weather to secure rations against the brutality of the coming miserable season.

To James, the ripening chestnuts heralded more than just the return of winter. It also meant that it was once again time for him to return to subsidiary. James had not worried about his uncomfortable confrontation with Barba Peyrot for several weeks. Antoinette's counsel had brought him comfort, allowing him to put the experience out of his mind. But as his return to subsidiary grew nearer, James once again found himself growing anxious.

Jabez Woodard paid the family a visit a few days prior to when James would have to face his teacher. It was an overcast and miserably gray day. The wind tossed the tree branches back and forth all across the mountainside as Jabez carefully made his way up the family lane toward their cottage.

Jabez looked uncharacteristically concerned as he entered their home. This worried look grew all the more anxious as he took a seat upstairs. Jabez looked at Papa and nervously began, "Jean, Brigham Young has asked that all converts immigrate to the Deseret Territory." He paused to give his words time to sink in. "We have been asked to help every family prepare to make this journey."

"What does immigrate mean?" James asked.

"It means that they want you to all move to America!" Marguerite responded, her voice dripping with venom. "Can you imagine?   Our family, move to America?" she continued disgustedly. "I told you. And now look what you have all gotten yourselves into!"

"We cannot afford to move to America," Papa said thoughtfully.

"Good," replied Marguerite. "The Mormons will all leave the valleys, and our life can get back to normal.

"There is a way that you can purchase fare to America for your entire family. It will not be easy, and will require tremendous sacrifice on the part of your family," Jabez paused, struggling to find the courage to continue. "Under the Lord's inspiration Brigham Young has prepared a fund called the Perpetual Immigration Fund. The Church will loan your family the money that you need to move to Deseret. And you can pay it back by working for the Church after you arrive."

Jabez again hesitated. "You would, of course, have to pay as much of your own fare as you can before the Church will be able to help you. This will mean selling your farm, along with everything else that you own."

Selling the farm was an almost unthinkable act. It had preserved their family since the 1600s. It was the family's only means of survival. Their only insurance that they would have food to eat. James was certain that Papa would be unwilling to sell it.

Marguerite echoed James sentiment, "Sell the farm! Papa! You might as well sell our surname!" These comments were not far off. A farm was as much of a person's identity as was their name. Although James supposed that if they did indeed move to America, a farm in Italy would not do them much good. It was all too much for James to process.

First, he had learned that God had called a prophet. Then, he had had to disappoint his favorite teacher. And now, the Lord was asking them to sell the family's farm and move away from the valleys. But not only from the valleys, but all the way to America!

"I know that this is a difficult commandment, but remember, Brother Jean, it is a commandment from the Lord. He will help us, if we do all that we can." Jabez continued, "We will be traveling to Deseret in groups. The first group will leave in February. I have come to ask your family to be a part of that first group."

Papa thoughtfully considered the matter. He hesitantly looked around the room at each of his children before replying. He then looked Jabez Woodard directly in the eyes and said, "Brother Jabez, if this is the Lord's will, then we will sell our farm, and together, we will travel to America."

The mood in the room was that of somber faith. To leave their valleys seemed an unimaginable, unthinkable thing. It was not something that their people did. It was simply not in their blood. Their ancestors had fought to remain here, to preserve their lands. Many had died so that they could hold onto their farms. That the Lord would ask this of them was beyond the possibility of thought. While most of them kept these feelings quietly to themselves, Marguerite was beside herself. "Papa, you cannot sell the farm! How will we survive winter?"

"Sweetheart, owning a farm in the valleys will not make any difference to us if we are far away in Deseret," Papa gently answered, clearly worried that he would further upset her. But at the same time trying to help her see the logic of their situation.

"And what then, Papa? How will we survive in that . . . that . . . horrible land?" she cried. "Surrounded by Mormons, who ask you to give them everything! And don't care that the result is you then have nothing! Worse than nothing! We will owe them money. You heard Jabez, Papa. We will have to work as their servants."

The timber of Marguerite's voice climbed, reaching a pitch

that resembled the sound that a crow makes when it gets stuck in a fence. "Papa, we don't even speak the same language. We will be outsiders with no farm, no money, no place to sleep, and no friends!" She paused in order to calm herself down, then continued in a more resolute tone. "Papa, I won't go! I won't leave the valleys!"

Marguerite's mood remained one of absolute misery for the next several weeks. She spent as little time at home as possible. When she was there, she spoke to her family only briefly, and in tones that made her disdain for them evident.

James, it turned out, did not return for his final season of subsidiary. Papa felt that his energy could better be utilized by working alongside his brothers to prepare their farm to be sold. They labored hour after hour, day after day, repairing everything, from the recently broken, to the long neglected. Together they tried their best to return everything to pristine condition. They hoped that this would allow them to negotiate the highest possible price for their meager lands.

During Sabbath afternoons, James was able to wander short distances from their home. The valleys now looked more beautiful than they ever had before. The snows of winter once again graced the landscape with its rocky precipices. James marveled at the sight. He was sure that America couldn't possibly be this beautiful. Did they even have snow there? James decided that he had better enjoy these last few weeks, and try his best to forever record the scenes of his home deep into his memory. He lamented the fact that he would never again get to live in sacred valleys surrounded by towering mountains. According to Jean, who had read stories about America, it was a strange land full of vast rivers, Indians, and dry deserts, none of which sounded very appealing to James.

By December, Papa had found a buyer for their land. It was not often that a farm went up for sale in the valleys. These inheritances were typically passed down from father to son. But even despite the scarcity of land, Papa was still only able to fetch 2,200 lire. Far less than they had hoped. Perhaps if they had had more time they could have gotten more money. But their need to sell was urgent. In order to complete the sale, it would be necessary for Papa to travel some fifteen miles through deep snows to meet the buyer and exchange the deed.

"Papa, you are sixty four years old. You cannot travel in this weather. I will make the journey," Jean protested.

"Son, I have to go. The deed is in my name. I have to be

the one to sign the documents," Papa countered.

"Then let me go with you," Jean offered.

In the end, it was decided that Jean and Papa would travel together. The journey there and back would take them at least three days.

Antoinette, Marguerite, and James would remain at home alone, while Daniel had a journey of his own that he would have to undertake. One much more difficult than that of Papa and Jean's.

Daniel was now eighteen years old. As a citizen of Savoy, he was required to be available to serve in the King's military, should his name be drawn from a lottery. It was possible to purchase an exemption from this lottery, but doing so was typically beyond the means of what ordinary citizens could afford. Buying an exemption was meant to be a privilege reserved for the sons of wealthy aristocrats and nobility.

If Daniel were to be allowed to travel with the rest of their family to America, he would first have to be freed from this obligation. Borrowing 200 lire from the Pons family, who had recently sold their own farm, Daniel headed to La Torre, a journey of several miles. Once there, he would use this money to purchase his freedom. When Papa and Jean returned, they would use a portion of the funds from the sale of their farm to repay Daniel's debt to the Pons family. The remaining funds, which were nowhere near sufficient to secure passage for all of them to America, would then be given to Jabez Woodard.

Papa signed a contract with the Church which guaranteed his family the remaining funds that were needed for their trip to America. These funds would be drawn from the Mormon Church's Perpetual Immigration Fund. This contract further stipulated that Jean and his sons would be required to work this debt off upon their arrival in Deseret. The Lord had indeed provided a way for them to follow his commandment to move to Deseret. However, they would have no property or money with which to start their new life once they arrived. And before they could earn any, they would first have to work off their debt to the Church.

Marguerite's warnings now seemed to be validated. They would arrive in America as beggars. No money, no farm, no friends, and completely unable to speak the language. James was truly terrified by the prospect. But they moved forward with faith, nevertheless. Except for Marguerite, who still insisted that she would not be going with them.

1854

Chapter Thirteen

Leaving the Valleys

Never in anyone's memory had there been a time of such anticipation in the valleys. It seemed that people everywhere were excitedly preparing for the coming celebrations. This was especially true in the valley basins, where temples, schools, and the markets were all filled with the chatter of restless villagers.,

The Waldensians did not usually have time for fruitless activities such as balls, parties, and the like. Nor could they easily afford to spare the extra food that such celebrations usually called for. But in this case, the people felt that the festivities were warranted.

In each temple, a special sermon was to be preached. An assigned barba would stand and remind the villagers of the struggles and turmoil that the Waldensians have faced over the centuries. Another barba would then take the podium and extol the righteousness of their Sovereign, His Majesty, King Charles Albert, the Ruler of Sardinia.

It had been six years since King Charles had issued the Edict of Emancipation, granting the Waldensians the legal right to worship according to the dictates of their own hearts. Similar promises had been made by other rulers over the centuries. A promise of freedom, if the Waldensians would just but lay down their defensive weapons, and back away from their watch towers. However, in each of these previous instances, the Waldensians had been betrayed, usually at the cost of many of their lives. At first, when these offers of peace had been extended, the people of the valleys had eagerly laid down their weapons. And then, although they had been promised protection, their deceitful rulers had instead sent in military forces to invade the naturally fortified mountains, which had for so long allowed this people to frustrate the most powerful armies of Europe.

It had taken the Waldensians generations, and multiple

betrayals, but at last, they had learned to be more cautious of such offers. For the first few years after their Sovereign King had issued the Edict of Emancipation in 1848, the Waldensians remained understandably wary, ready to defend themselves against the expected attack. But as the years passed, and the soldiers never came, the number of alpine mountaineers who had hope began to swell. Perhaps this time things would really be different. February 17th would mark six years of anxious quiet. Six years of peace. It now seemed that the King's offer was genuine, and the barbes had decided it was time to rejoice in the glory of their ruler. They felt that the resounding music of freedom should be sung from the valley floors to the tops of the mountains.

After the people had gathered together, and the sermons had been preached, neighbors would then join for a feast. On the menu would be bread, a small piece of meat, and a bit of fruit. Hardly enough food to impress those who lived in wealthier nations, but it was more than many of these impoverished mountaineers ate in an entire day. After their feast, the people would then march together through the streets, cheering and praising King Charles.

The evening would then end with the most impressive

display of bonfires imaginable. The mountains themselves would appear as though they were alive. Enough of these fires were planned that it would be impossible for a person to look in any direction without seeing less than a dozen of them.

It was a day that was meant to be more spectacular and wonderful than any Waldensian had experienced in a thousand years. And it was all Marguerite could do to contain her excitement, even though the festivities were still two months away. In the meantime, she had important preparations to attend to. Most pressing of these was the matter of her room and board. She had to find a place to live after her family left the valleys. Her Family! They should be taking care of her! But instead, they were more interested in their silly new religion.

Marguerite had grown tired of arguing with Papa, who not only refused to give up Mormonism, but actually wanted her to consider joining him in his apostasy. Her brothers and sister were no better. It was as if all of them had decided to join up against her.

She had tried to persuade them away from their budding beliefs, but they simply refused to see reason. If they wanted to look like fools to the rest of the village, then that was their own business. She was through trying to help them.

Marguerite was especially furious with Papa for having sold the farm. And then, to make matters worse, he had wasted the money on passage to America, including fare for her, even though she had made it clear that she was not going. Why couldn't he have at least let her keep her share of the proceeds? This would have given her something to start a new life with. But it didn't matter. Even without a farm or money, Marguerite had many friends whom she was confident would assist her.

A milder than usual winter had allowed Marguerite the pleasure of making short treks in order to visit some of these dear friends. People who appreciated her, and who understood all that she had to endure, being as she was, the daughter of an apostate family.

Marguerite fumed at the inconsideration of her family as she hiked along the trails that led to the home of Louisa. Look how dirty my beautiful dress is getting. She thought to herself. And her feet were so cold. "How could they be so thoughtless? All they care about is their ridiculous Mormon Church." she mumbled outloud.

Louisa's Papa invited Marguerite into their home, which

was in almost every regard identical to that which Marguerite had been raised in. Except that the lower floor, where the animals were kept, was dug halfway into the mountainside, and the upper floor where the family lived also had an outside entrance that met the mountain as it ran sharply up toward the sky.

Marguerite took a seat in the upstairs living area, along with Louisa, her little brother, and her Mama and Papa. After exchanging pleasantries, she launched into a tale of her abuses at the hands of her family. How they had sold everything they owned, and would now be leaving on a fool-hearty journey to who knew where. She recounted how they had all been taken in by Mormon charlatans; predators from America who had convinced them to undertake such foolish endeavors.

None of this prattle was news to her hosts. They had on many occasions invited Marguerite in to share stories of her family. Indeed, these neighbors had come to look forward to Marguerite's visits. The gossip was of such a scandalizing nature that it brought welcome entertainment to the dreary winter boredom.

Today, Marguerite intended to do more than just recount her many injustices. Today, she also meant to ask Louisa's Papa to help her. She believed that these friends clearly understood and appreciated her situation. After all, they had on many occasions commented about how unfortunate her family was.

After updating them on the latest news regarding her family's plans to leave the valleys, Marguerite paused. She adorned her face with a pathetic and pleading look, and then carefully addressed Louisa's Papa, Peter.

"You have been so kind to me in my time of need." Marguerite thought that it was important to begin her request by assuring Peter that she was grateful for all their kindness. They had not fed her, or given her any material goods, but the bond of friendship between them had been strong, and that was kindness enough.

"Indeed, you have shown me more charity than I deserve. Given my family connections, I feel almost as though I were one of your daughters." Marguerite looked at Peter. "I have grown to consider you more of a Papa to me than a mere friend," she paused for dramatic effect.

"I don't know how I would survive without friends like you." She again looked at Peter, "I had hoped that by now you might also consider me a daughter."

As the purpose of her words began to dawn on Peter, his

look of pity for the girl began to change into a look of uncomfortable panic.

"What I mean to ask," continued Marguerite, "is if you would be willing to allow me to become a part of your family," she concluded.

Marguerite felt that she had asked the question perfectly. She had sounded humble and gracious. She had looked in Peter's eyes at the right moments and then down at the floor when she felt it would be appropriate to look needy. Marguerite was absolutely certain of the answer she would receive.

"Marguerite, child!" laughed Peter. "We cannot take you on! What a ludicrous idea. We barely have enough for those of us already here. How, dear, would we also feed you?"

Silence. Marguerite had not expected them to tell her no, let alone laugh at her. It was insupportable. What horrible people! After all the hours they had spent discussing her family. She had confided in them. And now they had the audacity to not only turn her away, but to also laugh at her!?

Shocked, Marguerite stood up, looked around the room at each member of Louisa's family, doing her very best to make sure that her face showed the disgust that she felt toward them. She then walked out, slamming the door behind her.

Just wait until she got to her friend Elizabeth's house. They would enjoy learning what terrible people Louisa and her family were. Elizabeth, Marguerite realized, had been the truer friend all along.

ဢ

"Jabez! What a wonderful surprise. Please, come in," Papa invited.

The unusually temperate winter, along with the necessity of preparing for their trek to Deseret, had the effect of bringing more visitors to their home than was typical during this time of year.

"What brings you our way, Brother Woodard?" asked Papa, after Jabez had had an opportunity to make his way upstairs and take a seat in one of the rickety old chairs.

"Jean, I have come with news of our journey to Deseret. As you know, coordinating such an undertaking has not been easy. But we have at last worked out many of the finer details. Do you have time to discuss some of these?" asked Jabez.

Papa chuckled, "Time is something that we have plenty of right now Jabez. Please, go on," he gestured with his hand.

Jabez smiled, "Yes, indeed, I am still getting used to these alpine winters. Well then, your family, along with the Pons family and the Cardon family will make up the first group. The nineteen of you will leave the valleys on the seventh of February..."

"The seventh of February? But we will miss the celebrations!" interrupted James. Even though he knew he was leaving the valleys, he had still looked forward to taking part in the valley-wide extravaganzas. He had come to think of them as a sort of sending off party for his family. As if the entire Waldensian community were coming together to wish them all a safe journey.

"I am sorry, son," replied Jabez, who could not fully appreciate what it meant to the young impoverished boy to see such grandeur, having spent most of his life in London where these kinds of events were far more common, and on a much grander scale. "But our ship leaves port on the twelfth of March. If you do not leave on the seventh, then you will not have enough time to travel to England."

"You will first all travel to Geneva, Switzerland. Here you will be met by Thomas Stenhouse. Thomas will then conduct you to Liverpool, England."

"And what about you, Jabez?" inquired Papa. "I thought you were to travel with us."

"Indeed, but I have to travel ahead of you. I will meet you all in Liverpool. We have already paid your fares on a ship called the John M. Wood. But if someone is not there at least one week prior to the ship's departure, then they will sell our tickets. I am going to travel ahead and make sure they know the rest of you are indeed on your way."

Already purchased their passage? These words had a jarring effect on James, waking him up to the reality of what was about to happen. He knew they were leaving, however, it had not yet truly seemed real.

True, they had already sold their home, but they were still living in it. This had allowed James' mind to pretend that nothing had changed. But now, they had booked passage on a ship. A ship that was headed away to an exotic part of the world where everything would be different.

This is my life. This is my future. We really are leaving our precious valleys, never to return again. We are going to a strange new land with Indians and who knew what else.

"This ship is supposed to be a good one, Jean. It has crossed the Atlantic many times. It will bring us to a city in America called New Orleans. From there, we will travel by foot to Deseret." Jabez paused, noticing that Marguerite was not in the home. He then asked, "Jean, what about your daughter, Marguerite? Has she changed her mind?"

This question brought a tremendous sorrow to Papa's face. "She says she will not be going. She hardly talks to any of us anymore. Instead, she spends as much time as possible in the company of friends. We may have to leave her behind," concluded Papa, with frank sadness.

It was difficult for James to see Papa in so much pain. How could Marguerite do this to him? How could she put him in such distress?

"Jean, I think we ought to hold a special fast for her," Jabez paused, "and for you," he added. "I still have to visit the Pons and Cardon families. I will invite them to join in this fast. Whatever happens, you are doing the right thing."

The next few weeks were especially difficult for James. While his neighbors prepared for a once in a lifetime gala, where they would celebrate their eternal commitment to the valleys, he and his family were preparing to forever leave this faithful rocky fortress.

Everywhere people spoke of the mountains with admiration, remarking on how they had protected their ancestors. They reminded each other that God himself had given these mountains to them and that they would be theirs for eternity. These comments stung James deeply. They would not be his for eternity, nor for many more weeks even. Shortly he would leave them all behind. Just when the battle of his people's liberation had at last been won. When it finally looked as though he and his children and his children's children could live here unburdened by the constant threat of attack from outsiders. After a thousand generations that his forefathers fought and died for the rights that had now just recently been granted to them. And how was his family expressing their gratitude to these many generations of brave defenders of the valleys? Not though celebration. No. Instead, they would in effect be saying to them, "We don't care about the valleys. Your sacrifices don't matter to us. We are moving away." James knew that he was following the commandments of a prophet. But he couldn't help but wonder why following a prophet had to be so difficult.

&

Marguerite was furious with her friends. One by one, they had all rejected her. She had employed all her crafts, from her most adorable expressions, to her charming wit. In every case, these so-called friends had been willing to listen to her as she gossiped about her family. But then, when it came time to help her, they had all turned their backs. Each had claimed that they could not afford another mouth to feed. That they were barely getting by as it was. Marguerite believed they were all selfish, horrible people.

Her friends had not helped, but she still had options. Marguerite determined that she would visit with the barbes. They would take compassion on her. Hadn't she been faithful in attending temple services all throughout the warm season, even after her family had stopped going? Barba Peyrot had visited their home, and had seen the pitiful manner by which her family had been deceived. He had said that she had a beautiful spirit. He, of all people, would help her get what she wanted.

Despite the fact that few made the trek to temple this time of year, Marguerite set out on the difficult hike. It would take all day to get there and back, but she needed to discuss the matter with Barba Peyrot himself. After several hours of walking in the cold, wet snow, she arrived at the lonesome temple.

"Marguerite, child! What are you doing all the way down here at this time of year?" Barba Peyrot said in astonishment, as he placed a warm blanket around her.

It was difficult to keep the temple warm. A small fire helped, but it was still necessary to remain bundled up.

"Barba, I have come to throw myself upon your bountiful charity. My family plans to leave for America with several other Mormons. I do not want to go with them. But I have no means to support myself once they are gone."

"Leaving for America!" Barba Peyrot was beside himself. "Why would they think to do such a fool-hearty thing?"

"The Mormons believe that God has commanded them to all move to a place in America called Deseret," Marguerite said disgustedly. "They think God is gathering all his . . . faithful there. Gathering the simpletons is more like it."

"But child, regardless of what they may desire to do, they can't possibly afford such a journey. I think you are making a bigger deal out of this than it really is. They are just putting on a show. Once they realize that they don't have the resources for such a journey, they will give up these silly notions."

"They have already purchased their passage to America. They leave in a couple weeks," Marguerite replied, looking Barba Peyrot straight in the eyes.

"How is this possible? There isn't a family within twenty miles that has enough money for such a trip," Barba Peyrot asked in shock.

"Papa sold our farm."

"What!" Barba Peyrot stood up. "Sold your farm! Child, then they really do mean to go through with this. And you have come seeking my help? Yes, of course, we can find you a new home. I will make all the arrangements."

80

James had been standing beside Mama's grave for a couple of hours now. In a few weeks they would leave her behind. He knew it was silly, but he felt like he would also be leaving her behind. Like somehow her spirit would be trapped in the mountains, unable to follow them to America.

"James, I have something for you.   Come inside." Antoinette's words startled James. He had not seen her walk up. She tenderly placed an arm across James' shoulders. Seeming to read his mind, she said, "She will be with us James. I think she is proud of you!"

The two of them walked inside together.

Jabez had instructed everyone to pack light. It was a long journey and it would be too difficult to lug heavy items with them. Each person had been given a small duffel bag which they could use to pack any personal belongings that would fit inside.

"James, before Mama died, she made a little blanket to wrap you in. When you grew too big for it, I put it away. It has been one of my most treasured possessions. It is the very last thing I remember her making. But it is not mine, it is yours. I hope you don't mind James, but I have sewn it into a shirt for you. I had to use some additional cloth because there was not enough, but most of it is made from Mama's blanket. I thought this way, when you wear it, it would be like she was hugging you."

James was overwhelmed. This material, which Mama had made, and which Antoinette had fashioned into a shirt, was the most wonderful thing that anyone had ever given him.

James could not speak, nor did he need to. Seeing his emotion, Antoinette opened her arms. James rested his head on her chest as she closed her arms around him, and he silently cried.

ৡ

It was a particularly long and difficult hike to get to the apparently abandoned home. Marguerite thought that this horrible farm was hardly worthy of the effort it had taken her to get here to see it.

The home was in poor repair. It looked as though it had not been properly maintained in years. There weren't any animals, and the crop field and gardens also bore signs of abandonment. Why would Barba Peyrot ask her to travel here?

"Ah, Marguerite," said Barba Peyrot as he gestured through the open door for her to come into the house."

"Michel, this is the young lady I have been telling you about."

The man that Barba Peyrot referred to as Michel was as

poorly groomed as was his farm. His clothes were dirty, as though they had not been washed in a long time. His hair was wild. And he seemed to carry the odor of too many months of accumulated filth.

Marguerite could overlook all of this. But there was something more that bothered her about the man. It was the way he looked at her as though she were a prized mule on the auction block.

Michel did not say anything in response to Barba Peyrot's introduction. Instead, he simply nodded, and continued to stare at Marguerite through greedy eyes.

"Um, yes, well, and Marguerite, this is Michel," continued Barba Peyrot.

Marguerite, smiled, and then looked at Barba Peyrot. "Why have you asked me here, Barba?"

"My dear, this is where you will be living," replied Barba Peyrot.

"You mean, I will be living here with Michel and his wife?" she asked.

Barba Peyrot paused uncomfortably, then continued, "You

will be living with Michel as his wife."

℘

During Marguerite's frequent absences, James had taken over responsibility for preparing the family's meals. He did not particularly enjoy cooking, but at least it gave him something to take his mind off their impending journey, which was now less than two weeks away.

Papa looked older to James than he ever had before. Planning for their expedition was stressful enough, but the thought of leaving one of his children behind seemed to be aging him further every day. James was impressed by Papa's faith. Despite his concern for Marguerite, he continued to prepare for the day when he would, out of obedience, leave his valleys and his daughter forever behind.

Jean and Daniel would not allow Papa to exert too much energy. They too could see that his broken heart was sapping his strength. Under Papa's direction, they made the final repairs to their home and farm that they had agreed with the buyer that they would make. Jean and Daniel also settled all the family's open accounts, and acquired the necessary items they would need for their trip.

James was just about to inform the rest of the family that their lunch was ready when Marguerite unexpectedly entered the upstairs room where they were seated. She fell onto her hay mattress, and defeatedly announced, "I am going with you to America." Her voice sounding resentful.

Only Papa had the presence of mind to react. The rest of them were stunned into silence. He scooped her off the floor and held her in his arms. Although she did not resist his attention, she also did not return his affection. After a few long seconds, he pulled back from her and asked, "What has brought this change, my dear?"

"It doesn't matter. Isn't it enough that I am going with you?" She walked away from Papa and leaned against the opposite wall. She then continued speaking, "I want to be baptized a Mormon," she stated flatly.

No one knew what to say. Was this really Marguerite? How could such a miraculous change have taken place? Just this morning she had left their home defiantly, insisting that she didn't need any of them. She had claimed that she had made arrangements for her own welfare. When she had walked out of their home, she had warned them that she may not even return that night. She was off to finalize the arrangements of where she would be living, and that if they wanted anything to do with her, they would forsake their dreadful new religion. And now, just a few hours later, she was not only asking to go with them to America, but also suggesting that she wanted to join the Mormon Church?

"Well?" she said impatiently. "I said that I want to be baptized."

Recovering himself, Papa gently asked, "Marguerite, sweetheart, I am so happy that you will be coming with us, and grateful that you want to be baptized. How is it possible that you have found a testimony between this morning and now?"

"A testimony? Of the Mormon Church? Don't be absurd. No, I certainly do not have a testimony, but I am not going to be the only one in Deseret who is not Mormon."

Marguerite was baptized on the first of February, one week prior to the rapidly approaching day of their departure. After the baptismal service, Jabez Woodard accompanied the family back to their home.

Once inside, Jabez looked at Papa for a few minutes, appearing as though he were trying to work up the courage to say something uncomfortable. Finally, Jabez began to nervously speak, "Jean, there is a matter that I need to discuss with you."

In an effort to put Jabez more at ease, Papa smiled and replied, "Jabez, what can you possibly have to say that would make you so nervous? You have asked us to give up everything that we own," Papa chuckled, "everything we are, for that matter. And we have been obedient. Certainly you can't have something on your mind that is more difficult to say than what you have already asked of us."

Jabez hesitated, then, looking at Papa, he said, "As you know, Jean, I will be traveling with your family to Deseret. While this allows me to watch over those families that are traveling, it creates a bit of a problem." Jabez paused for a moment.

"Those who remain behind will be left without a leader. It will be several months before the next group leaves for Deseret, and someone needs to be here to officiate in church meetings. Jean, without a leader, they may all fall into apostasy. We need someone to oversee the work until the next group is ready to leave. I have prayed to know the Lord's will, and I feel impressed that he wants you to serve as the Branch President here in the valleys."

Jabez repeated himself to be sure he was being understood, "The Lord wants you to remain here, Jean, to look after the Saints until they are all ready to leave for Deseret. You will then travel with them, in about a year's time."

James wasn't sure if he should be relieved or disappointed. They would get to spend another year in their valleys? Another year on their farm? But then James remembered that they no longer owned their farm. How would the family survive? Where would they all live?

"Where will we live, Papa?" James asked.

Jabez answered "James, you five will still need to leave next week. We have already spent your money to purchase passage across the Atlantic. We cannot afford to let that go to waste."

What did he mean that the five of them would still be leaving next week? Leave without Papa? Travel thousands of miles to the other side of the world alone? It was unfathomable. James absolutely would not endure such a trial.

"Jabez," responded Papa after several minutes of silence, "if this is the Lord's will, then we will be obedient."

1854

Chapter Fourteen

Across the Dreary Wilderness

As was the custom among his people, James had grown up with the expectation that he would commit the bible to memory. Accomplishing this required years of effort and study. James had begun learning the stories of the scriptures before he could even read, almost before he could walk. One of the epics that James most enjoyed was that of Moses and the Israelites.

It was a sensational tale, full of all the elements that made for a truly great adventure. As James had listened to the passages about their liberation from the Egyptians, he had always imagined that the Israelites must have been happy to leave Egypt. It must, he had thought, have been an exciting and joyful time for a people who had been kept in captivity for so many generations.

After four hundred years of slavery, this chosen people were finally leaving the painful snap of their taskmasters' whips behind. No longer subject to the will of others, they were free to set out toward a new land that God had prepared for them. A land where they could set their own future, and worship the one true God as they saw fit.

It had never occurred to James that leaving Egypt might have instead caused these former slaves to feel profound sorrow. He had not ever considered the homes they might have built in Egypt, with their associated gardens and orchards.

Moses was leading them away from the only place that they had ever known. Out into a dreary wilderness. To them, Palestine was as distant and foreign of a land as it was to the Egyptians. A place where their ancient forefathers had once lived, but a very long time ago. Why did they have to leave their homes in Egypt? Why couldn't the Lord simply banish the Egyptians to Palestine and allow the Israelites to remain along the fertile shores of the nile instead?

As James and his family left the sanctuary of their pristine alpine valleys, he gained a new appreciation and perspective on how these Israelites must have really felt.

James' heart was overcome with pain, swallowed up in grief that to him seemed unbearable. The weight of losing everything that he had ever loved felt like it was crushing him. The sensation was no different than as if a mountain goat had been jumping up and down on his chest. Each pounce deflating a little bit more of his will to continue onward.

James would never see his home again; that wonderful stone cottage that his family had lived in for five generations. A tiny fortress that had protected his ancestors from many difficult winters, and that had lent the security of its walls against the danger of frequent invaders.

James knew that they would be building a new home in Deseret. But it would not be the same. Deseret, after all, was not in the Piedmont valleys. As Papa's youngest son, James had always known that he would not inherit their family farm. He knew that at some point he would have to move out. But when that time came, James had imagined that he would find a place close to home. Perhaps a nearby farm. Close enough that he could return home as often as he wanted. Leaving the mountains all together was something that he had never considered.

Deseret was a strange and distant place that for James only existed in the stories told by Jabez Woodard. This Mormon preacher had told them that Deseret was a desert situated on the shores of a vast salty lake. How do you water a farm with salty water? Who would want to live in such an intolerable and hostile land, where Indians attacked, and nothing grew?

James lamented that he would never again walk along the well worn alpine mountain trails, nor would his eyes ever again take in the amazing alpine vistas. He would be denied the spontaneous thrill of leaping from boulders as he tried to take flight with the eagles, or chasing the passing chamois along a ridge. He would never again partake of the fresh chestnuts with which the Lord had graciously covered their hilltops. Nor would he feast upon the spring mulberries, the juice turning his face and hands bright purple.

Like the people who followed Moses, James would be leaving a fertile land to go live in what could only be described as a desolate and dreadfully barren wasteland.

And what about his friend Henri? This last fall, James hadn't been able to attend subsidiary with the other boys his age.

His family had been too busy preparing for their journey. Had the Israelites left friends behind?   After living together for four hundred years, James supposed that at least some of the Israelite boys must have surely played with the Egyptians.   What friendships had been broken by their departure? Had they been able to say goodbye? Or, like James, did they simply vanish into the unknown, leaving no word of where they had gone?

James thought that he could probably have endured leaving all of these things behind. If only he did not also have to abandon his dear Papa. He wasn't entirely alone, however, he did have company. He was traveling with his four older siblings. The five of them were also accompanied by both the Cardon family as well as the Pons family. But none of these served as adequate substitutes for his Papa. James missed him. His longing so exquisite that James wanted to drop down on his side behind every passing tree or boulder that they passed and sob.

To James, each step forward seemed impossibly difficult. Why did his feet keep carrying him in the wrong direction farther and farther from home? Away from the confidence and protection that Papa would give him?

As the hours wore on, James grew angry at his feet. He

wondered why they betrayed his heart. They ought to be carrying him toward the valleys where Papa would surely scoop him up and make him feel better.

As the hours turned into days, the darkness that engulfed James pressed ever more heavily upon him, choking out the air, making it difficult for him to breathe. It was all too much for his young heart to bear.

The little group of immigrants had made their way across the Alps, and were now headed to Geneva, Switzerland.

Antoinette spent most of the journey divided between Daniel and James. Daniel was now eighteen years old. To James, he seemed strong, brave, and fearless. At times, James pretended that Daniel was Papa. Although it did not last long, the exercise did provide a few moments of occasional relief from his anguish.

Daniel was not much better off than was James. He depended upon their sister Antoinette for strength. Recognizing this, she made sure that she was available to him whenever his spirits seemed depleted. She was careful not to treat Daniel as a child. She no longer coddled him as she once had. In place of her warm embrace, she offered instead her encouraging and uplifting words and peaceful, calming smile.

When not buoying up Daniel, Antoinette was usually found walking alongside James, her arm draped across his neck, while she did her best to distract him with conversation, stories, and music.

Antoinette had been the only reason that James had ultimately agreed to part company with Papa. She had been the only one able to break the grasp that James had had around Papa's waist. James had meant to be brave. He had meant to be strong. But when it came time to leave home, all pretenses of maturity on his part were quickly forgotten. Instead of walking away from their farm with his dignity intact, he had left in a fit of tears. Antoinette had to practically drag him away.

James was ashamed of his actions that day. He had behaved like a child. What embarrassed him even more was the fact that even now, four days later, he was still acting like an infant.

James was grateful that Marguerite was not around much to taunt him. She spent most of her time with the girls from the Pons and Cardon families, except for Lydia Pons, who walked alongside James' older brother Jean. These four mischievous young ladies usually traveled a short distance from the rest of the group, far enough away as to remain just out of earshot. They passed their time wrapped up in their own conversations, ignoring the rest of the group entirely.   Even at a distance, the body language of Marguerite's three traveling companions betrayed their attempts to gain her approval.   Marguerite would occasionally point at someone outside of their little group. An individual whom she had not deemed important enough to walk with. She would then make a whispered comment to her three admiring friends, which James supposed was probably about how unattractive they were, or about how poorly they were dressed, or some other equally silly insight. The other three would then nod their heads in agreement and they would all giggle loudly. Anyone foolish enough to look in their direction for too long would be treated to a barrage of scornful expressions. When the routine of their journey forced them to mix company with the rest of the group, such as at mealtimes, they made life genuinely miserable. Complaints were never far from their lips. Their feet hurt. They were dirty. The men smelled. It wasn't fair that they had to live in fields and eat weeds like cattle.

During the first few days of their trip, Jean had attempted to quiet Marguerite. He had admonished her to stop complaining. "Marguerite, please. I know that you are not happy, but neither are any of the rest of us. Can you please stop bickering?!" he had begged.

Marguerite's reply made it clear that she had no intention of easing up on her campaign to get the family to return to their senses.

"Bickering! Is that what you call it? Am I the only one who has not completely lost her mind? Jean, you just admitted that you are not happy. And yet, like a fool, you still insist that we keep walking away from our home!"

"The Lord has called us to Deseret, Marguerite! How can we turn our backs on him? And once we arrive, we will rebuild our lives. We will work hard and buy all the comforts that we left behind," Jean attempted to reason.

"Jean, you really are dumb!" Marguerite announced in a voice that was purposely loud enough for everyone else in the group to overhear. "All of you are!" she said in a patronizing tone, now addressing the group at large. "I am traveling with a bunch of simple minded idiots. All of you so dumb that upon the word of a couple of American frauds, you have allowed yourselves to be tricked into leaving your farms so that you could run off and die in the middle of no where!" she shouted.

After this encounter, everyone did their best to keep their

distance from Marguerite, except, of course, for her three admirers.

These three were not as vocal as was Marguerite in their complaining. At times, it seemed to James that they did not agree with her at all. When she was not around, they could be absolutely human, sometimes even pleasant. When Marguerite was taken away by a chore or off by herself attending to personal matters, the other three girls sometimes forgot that they were unhappy. They became almost tolerable as traveling companions. But Marguerite was never gone for long, and when she returned, the other girls quickly fell back into line. Faithfully supporting her efforts to make everyone else regret their decision to leave the Piedmont valleys.

80

"Are you alright, Jean? Do you want to talk?"

Jean thought that everyone else had already gone to bed. Unable to sleep, he had decided to walk over and sit beside the dwindling fire. He shivered as he sat on the frozen dirt next to the glowing embers. He probably should have thrown some more wood on the fire, but he was too lost in his thoughts to bother.

Which was probably a good thing. The sudden and unexpected sound of Lydia's voice startled Jean, causing him to jump. Had there been a roaring fire, he may have been burned.

Jean blushed, partly from his embarrassment at having jumped so high, and partly because he always seemed to blush in her presence.

"Wow!" she smiled. "You ought not be alone at night if you are that frightened of the dark!"

Even in the dark, Lydia was beautiful. Covered in a week's worth of dirt, with unkempt hair, and dirty clothes, somehow she managed to glow. Having her friendship made the present journey much more endurable.

"I had the hiccups," Jean smiled back at her.

"I see," she said, very seriously. "Well then, you had better hold your breath and drink some water."

After a few quiet moments sitting beside Jean, Lydia spoke again. This time in a less playful, more serious tone. "Jean, I mean it. Do you want to talk? I am worried about you. Everyday you look more tired, but every night you sleep less."

Jean did not respond immediately. He didn't know what to

say. He was not entirely certain he knew what was bothering him. Even if he could pinpoint his feelings, he was not sure how he felt about sharing them with his friend. He did not want to sound like he was complaining. He didn't want to appear weak in her eyes.

"I am alright. I suppose I am just not used to sleeping on the ground," he finally offered.

Jean felt Lydia's hand slip into his own, each of her soft fingers intertwining between his. He had never held a girl's hand in such an intimate way before. He had held Mama's hand, and the hands of his little sisters, but this was different. Although she was just a friend, the sensation of holding Lydia's hand seemed to erase the rest of the world around them, leaving just the two of them alone in the world.

"Jean, it is not your fault," Lydia whispered. "Marguerite is an individual free to make her own choices. You can't allow yourself to carry her guilt."

Jean was stunned. He had not said anything to Lydia about Marguerite. Not even to himself. Yet Lydia's words carried a profound and immediate impact upon his heart. She was right. This is what had been bothering him, although he himself had not understood it.

He was the oldest of his siblings. In Papa's absence, it was his responsibility to care for the family. The actions of each of his younger brothers and sisters reflected on him. If any of them became injured either physically or spiritually on this journey, it would be his fault.

Although he had not verbalized this reality before this moment, now that Lydia had pointed it out, he could not deny that this is what was bothering him. It was almost too much to bear. Not just Marguerite, but all of them. Traveling across the world was a dangerous business. People died on these types of trips all the time. Jean had read about such voyages in books. The world outside of their valleys was a dangerous place. Accidents, disease, crime. Around every corner a new potential danger awaited his family. And it all came down to him and his ability as their big brother to protect them.

Lydia was right that his preoccupation at present was Marguerite. Her headstrong unwillingness to listen to anyone. Her apparent disgust with everyone and everything, especially the Mormon Church.

Jean knew that he could not force her to gain a testimony of the family's new faith. Such a thing was deeply personal. It could only be found as he himself had found it, by personally seeking to know for ones own self, in prayer. He could not very well hold Marguerite down and force her to pray, though he wished that he could. If she knew how real the testimony was that he had received, Jean was sure that she would not complain so much. It was not just an imagined feeling in his heart. It was deep and abiding. It was substantial and undeniable. It was as tangible and real as was Lydia's hand.

Jean knew that he was not to blame for Marguerite's refusal to accept the gospel. But this did not ease his concern for her, nor did it make him feel any less responsible for her. However, as he sat holding Lydia's hand, he felt for the first time in nearly a week a great sense of relief. Not because he felt any less responsible, but because he now understood what was bothering him. And more importantly, because he was not alone. Lydia understood the weight he carried, and somehow that made him feel as though he were not carrying it alone.

1853

Chapter Fifteen

Words of a Prophet

After a week of wandering together across the European countryside, Barthélémy Pons announced that on the following day they would at last pass through a city.

Geneva, Switzerland, wasn't just any city either. It had a long history of friendship with the Waldensian people. This stronghold of the Protestant Church had offered protection, shelter, and food to the Waldensians during times when outside armies had forced them to flee their mountain homes. The people of Geneva had also spearheaded many efforts over the centuries to collect books and other necessities for their mountain beneficiaries, sending them along with teachers who established schools for the people of the valleys.

James had been taught that the Swiss were a kind, wealthy, and God-fearing people, and he was excited to see the city that had given so much to the Waldensians.

"We will only have time to spend a few hours in Geneva," cautioned Barthélemy. "Just enough time for a meal and a brief night's rest."

"Yes, but it will be a very comfortable night," smiled Louise Cardon. "I have spent time there before. It is a magnificent place," he continued excitedly. "You will see buildings that rise toward the sky. More shops than you can imagine. And the best part, lots of great food!"

"Not to mention a soft bed," sighed Barthélemy, as he rubbed his back.

Buildings that rise toward the sky? James had heard about the buildings that stood in the great European capitals and how some of them rose four or five stories high. He imagined these buildings wobbling back and forth along with the trees in the wind. It must be terrifying to live so high off the ground. His mountains were high, but they were stable. They were part of the Earth and had been fashioned by the hands of God himself. These buildings were man made, like the Tower of Babel. Surely they would topple over at the first gust of wind, or at the slightest tremor of the ground.

As the group of eighteen travelers walked through the streets of Geneva, James marveled at what he saw. There were so many people coming and going. At times he could see as many as twenty people walking in and out of the various shops.

There were shops that had displays in the windows, showing off the most colorful dresses that James had ever seen. Shops that sold hats, shops that dealt in tobacco, or meat, or bread, or watches, or any number of other specialty items.

And then there were buildings that did not appear to have any shops at all. Men and women entered and left these buildings just as frequently as the shops. Jean explained that these were business offices, law firms, and factories.

Their night in Geneva lived up to everyone's expectations. Even Marguerite was more cheerful than usual. After feasting on a meal that consisted of enough food to have fed James for two or three days, James fell asleep on the softest bed he had ever slept on in his life, surrounded by a mountain of blankets and pillows, and kept warm all night by a glowing fire.

They arose early the next morning, and as quickly as they had entered Geneva, they left. With the memory of the luxuries of Geneva still on their minds, their journey now seemed all the more difficult. The first week had been hard, but just moderately more so than their dreary lives of poverty back home. They had never before experienced such luxury as they had in Geneva. Now somehow everything seemed doubly difficult.

It would be another two weeks before they would arrive in Paris, France. Between now and then they would have to spend fourteen more days sleeping as vagabonds in the countryside.

In Geneva, the group picked up forty three additional travelers. These Swiss converts were led by a thirty eight year old man named Thomas Stenhouse. Stenhouse would be leading the group the rest of the way to Liverpool, England. Barthélémy Pons appeared grateful to be able to hand command of the party off to Stenhouse. James supposed that he was probably tired of having to be responsible for Marguerite and her friends, one of which, Marie Pons, was his own daughter.

As the group set out under their new leader, Jean reminded

James that Thomas Stenhouse had, along with another man named Lorenzo Snow, preached together in their temple four years earlier. James was surprised to find that his spirits declined somewhat as he remembered that day. At the time, James had thought that these two American preachers were out of their minds. He had even felt embarrassed for them. But at the request of both his Papa and also Barba Peyrot, James had been respectful. He had carefully concealed his feelings, not allowing them to show on his face, except for a brief moment when they had preached about there being new scriptures. But James had quickly regained his composure and had erased his disbelief from his expressions.

James couldn't help but laugh bitterly to himself at the irony of their present condition. Four years had passed since that encounter, and James was once again in the company of this American preacher. Only this time James thought that Thomas Stenhouse was not the only one who was crazy. As they met again, James concluded that now he too had lost his mind.

Had it been a mistake to leave home? All that it had accomplished so far was to make him miserable. And from the looks of his brothers and sisters, they too seemed much worse for having left the valleys. Maybe they should have stayed home, under the watchful care of the barbes, safely on their farm. Life was not easy there, but it was certain and sure. As long as you worked hard you could survive. How does one survive in an American desert, farming lizards and eating cactus?

As James walked, he silently questioned his convictions. His testimony had never been as strong as his older brother Jean's, or as firm as Papa's. But James could not deny that he had felt a warmth at hearing the doctrines that the Mormon Missionaries taught. And he would never forget how that warmth had exploded within him on the night that he had had to face Barba Peyrot and choose between the Mormons faith, and that of the Waldensians. In that moment he had been absolutely sure of his choice. Had he been wrong? Had Marguerite been right? Is he, as Marguerite often accused him of being, a fool?

The longing for home, the pain of being away from Papa, these were bad enough. But the thought that they might be, as Marguerite had suggested, on a fool's errand! That it all might have been for nothing. It threatened to drown him in despair. If they were wrong, then shouldn't they turn around? Shouldn't they go home?

But they couldn't go home, could they? They didn't have a

home anymore. They had sold it, and had given all their money to the Mormons. If they turned around now they would have nothing. Nowhere to live, nothing to eat. Someone else now occupied their home. Someone else would be working their farm.

The group continued walking towards Paris. As the hours passed, James' remaining strength was torn to shreds with cruel and relentless brutality. The sun moved across a mostly cloudless sky, unnoticed by him. James lost track of the movement of his feet. Occasionally he became aware that he was still walking. He would look around at the foreign landscape, so different from home, and then retreat back into his depressed thoughts.

At times throughout the day he heard Antoinette's voice, but he didn't bother to answer her. He just kept methodically and thoughtlessly moving in the same general direction as the rest of the group.

At midday, when the group stopped to eat, James slumped against a tree and stared blankly out at the horizon. It was an ugly place, he thought to himself. Just a bunch of worthless hills. Nothing taller than a barn. Certainly nothing so majestic as the Alps in any direction as far as the eye could see.

"James, please eat something," he heard Jean say. He did

not respond.

"James, can I put some jam on your bread?" asked Antoinette a few minutes later.

It was a very kind gesture on her part to offer this. She had brought a small jar of homemade jam with her from home. She did not have very much of it, only enough to cover a few slices. James knew that she had been saving it. He managed to say, "No, thank you," and then obliged both of them by taking a small bite of his bread.

Lunch ended, and the group of sixty one travelers set out once again toward Paris. James began to regret skipping breakfast and eating only one small bite of bread for lunch, his hunger now adding to his misery. His pace slackened, allowing most of the group to pass him. His brothers Jean and Daniel and his sister Antoinette slowed their pace so that they remained at his side. They did not complain or tell him to hurry. They just walked patiently alongside him.

As the afternoon sun pressed down on James, he began to feel dizzy. He wanted so badly to return home. He was hungry, and most of all, he longed for the arms of Papa to hold him. He couldn't go any farther from home. Not one more step. But he knew he couldn't go back, either.   Finally, out of exhaustion, misery, and hunger he gave up and collapsed beside the trail that they had been following.

Antoinette, Daniel and Jean were at his side almost before he hit the ground. They had promised Papa that they would take care of their younger brother, and they were not about to fall short in that duty.

"Daniel," ordered Antoinette, her voice a mixture of both soothing calmness and also alarm, "fetch some water."

She slid her lap underneath James, tenderly placing his head on her leg. "James," she spoke softly, her mouth near enough to his face that he could feel her breath.

"Is he okay?" Daniel said, panting as he returned with a bowl of fresh water.

James felt embarrassed. They were all treating him like he was dying.

"James, do you feel sick?" asked Antoinette.

He didn't feel sick. He was hungry, but other than that, physically he felt fine. He had collapsed due to emotional weakness. He missed home. How could he explain that to his older and stronger siblings?

Because he did not answer right away, it was suggested by Daniel that Jean use his newly conferred priesthood to give James a blessing of healing.

James now began to feel rather uncomfortable. He could allow his family to think he was ill, but unlike his brothers and sister, the Lord knew the truth. That he was just weak in spirit, and not sick.

James wondered if it would be blasphemous to accept a blessing of healing when he didn't need one. But once again, James could not find any words to decline. Instead, he remained quietly still, with his head lying across Antoinette's skirt.

Jean laid his hands upon his little brother's head and began to speak, his voice sounding unsure. This was the first blessing that Jean had ever pronounced. He had heard blessings being administered, but only once or twice. And he had no training in how to give one properly.

"James, by the err . . . power of God, I bless you that you will recover . . . " Jean paused and then started over, this time sounding more confident.

"James, you are not alone. You are away from your father, this is true. But your Heavenly Father is with you. You do not see him, but he is here with you, and he loves you.

"Your Heavenly Father is proud of you. You have followed the voice of his prophet Brigham Young. You have been obedient. Well done, James! It was not easy, but you did it. You *are* doing it!

"Now get up. Keep moving forward. God will be with you in each step that you take." With that, Jean removed his hands from James' head.

James was shocked. How had Jean known exactly what was wrong with him? Everyone thought that James had been physically ill. Jean had begun his blessing with this same assumption, but then he altered course. Instead of pronouncing a blessing of healing for a pretended sickness, Jean had instead spoke the words that James had so desperately needed to hear; that he was not alone, and certainly not crazy. Jean had assured him that James was indeed following the commandments of a prophet. The trail still lay before him. The daunting journey had not been removed. But somehow it now seemed to James to be a much more manageable task.

James wondered if God had just been testing his resolve.

Had the Lord been waiting to see how far he would walk before he gave up? In his blessing, Jean had said that God was proud of him. Proud. Just like Papa was proud of him. Jean had also said that God would be with him in every step. The thought of having the Lord so close helped to dull the pain that had been circling about him. His longing and sadness were still there. But for the first time in more than a week, James once again felt hope.

James lifted his head from Antoinette's leg, feeling shyly awkward at the commotion that he had created. He looked at his brothers. Daniel and Jean grabbed his arms and helped him stand, and then they, along with Antoinette, embraced him, their tears flowing freely as they each expressed their love for their little brother.

As they tightly held on to one another, Marguerite glanced back at them. In amusement, she commented to her three friends, "At last! Look, girls, at my silly family. They are crumbling. Soon they will be ready to turn around and go home." She nodded in self-satisfaction.

Jean glanced at her, his expression one of regret. He tried to communicate across the distance that he wished that she too were in the arms of their present embrace. Marguerite misread his expression, choosing to believe instead that Jean was admiring her strength and regretting not listening to her when she had warned them to stay home.

"They are lucky to have me," she squealed to no one in particular. "We will return home soon, where everyone will see that Marguerite was the only smart one in this family."

Marguerite waved cheerfully at Jean, and then promptly turned on her heels and continued walking in the opposite direction. Let them all watch her walk away from them, she thought to herself. The only one with any strength or sensibility.

1854

Chapter Sixteen

The Leader

James' family eventually let him escape from their tangled arms, and the four of them set out once again, walking side by side the remainder of the day. James found that he was now able to be much more cheerful than he had been earlier in the day. As they walked, they sang songs, or passed the time tossing stones at various passing targets. The more he interacted with his family, the less he worried about the life they were leaving behind, or the unknown world they were traveling towards.

That night, as everyone laid down to go to sleep, James began to wonder what would have happened if the Mormon missionaries had not preached in their temple so many years earlier. Whereas earlier in the day he had been wondering whether or not his family had been foolish to listen to the Mormons, now he began to think about what they would have missed out on had they never encountered these preachers.

What if Jabez and Barthélémy had not found Daniel on the mountainside and subsequently brought him home? What if their family had never been baptized?

The realization that they very easily could have been overlooked by the Mormons scared James. He supposed that he could have lived out his life in the valleys amongst his people. But at what cost? To never have felt this spirit burn within him, and to have been kept from the knowledge that God had restored the fullness of his gospel upon the Earth? The Waldensian people treasured the scriptures. But so few of them would ever get to read the Book of Mormon; words written by ancient prophets on the American continents. And his people, the Waldensians, the self-described keepers of the light of the scriptures didn't even know about them.

James began to realize how selfish he had been. He had only been thinking about himself. He hadn't once considered the fate of the people that they had left behind. The mountains were full of Waldensians, most of whom had never heard the missionaries preach. Perhaps they too would have accepted the gospel message, if only they had been given the opportunity to hear it. And now it would be too late. The Mormons were all leaving. No one would be left to teach them.

These thoughts overwhelmed James as he lay on the hard cold ground. Fearing that he would wake Daniel or Antoinette, who were laying on either side of him, James carefully slid out of his blanket, and quietly crept away from the group into a nearby meadow where he could be alone.

All around him, James was treated to a spectacular show of the Lord's power. The beautiful trees, the crickets, the breathtaking stars in the heavens. It all testified to James that God loved his children.

James knelt down and began to pray. He asked the Lord to forgive him for allowing himself to succumb to the darkness of his misery. He asked God to help him remain strong and to bear him up under his afflictions. And he promised to serve the Lord.

James briefly paused before continuing his prayer. He opened his eyes and while looking up at the stars asked the Lord for permission to someday return to his people as a missionary. He asked that he be allowed to preach the gospel to those Waldensians who had not heard it when the missionaries had passed through the first time.

The next day James felt as though he were a new person. He felt changed. He was stronger, happier, and more anxious to continue on to their new promised land. Instead of needing Antoinette's constant attention, James now found within himself the capacity to be a strength to those around him.

෨

Thomas Stenhouse was a quiet and measured sort of leader. He did not appear to James to be particularly comfortable in the position that he found himself. His orders were given with an insecurity that seemed to ask permission rather than give direction.

"We will eat supper in that field just ahead, unless anyone thinks that we should continue farther?" Thomas softly proclaimed, pointing to a clearing alongside the road. "But that looks like as good a place as any," his voice trailed off uncertainly.

It was a pretty place with open grasses that ran up next to a small rocky stream. This stream was made all the more beautiful, being laden with ice as it was. It was small enough that the stream could be easily crossed with a few careful jumps, but big enough that it made a peaceful background noise while they ate.

No one objected to the location that Thomas had selected, and so the group made their way to the meadow and settled in. Once there, each family claimed a little spot of ground where they could prepare a meal for themselves.

Without Papa's influence to encourage her, Marguerite could no longer be bothered to fix the family's meals. This role, as a result, had fallen onto Antoinette's shoulders.

James helped her make a small fire, while Daniel skinned and gutted a squirrel he had caught the night before and that he had kept tied to the outside of his bag all day. A bit of meat would be a nice change from the usual scanty supper of mostly bread, nuts, and sparse fruits.

As Antoinette cooked, the heavenly scent of simmering meat wafted through the meadow and caught the attention of every other member of their group, who looked at them enviously. There was barely enough meat for the five of them, let alone any leftovers to share with anyone outside of their little family.

Marguerite, who was loath to spend anytime with the family, did not hesitate to loudly make her way toward them, now that they had something she wanted, and claim her portion of the meal.

No one objected. Indeed, they were all happy to have her sit with them for once, as long as their meal lasted. During the brief meal, they each did their best to make conversation with Marguerite in an effort to make her feel included in the family. She in turn mostly ignored them.

As soon as she finished her small portion of meat, which was slightly larger than that which anyone else got, she promptly stood up and left without saying a word of thanks or goodbye.

Thomas Stenhouse stood and moved towards the center of the meadow. He looked as though he were going to speak, but then remained silent. After a few moments of looking around the group, he finally found his voice, allowing him to say what was on his mind.

"I think that we should probably try and get a few more miles behind us before we settle in for the night," he announced. "If everyone feels up to some more walking, that is."

Within a few minutes everyone had cleaned up and

repacked their supplies. Once again they were back on the road, walking toward Paris.

Marguerite's temperament grew more miserable with each new day that her family did not give up and ask to return to the Alps. She had been sure that by now they would have all come to her, begging her to forgive them. Instead, they now seemed to be getting along better each day, and were more resolved than ever to continue in their journey to America.

Nothing pleased her. She was uncomfortable. She was too wet, too muddy, too hungry, too cold, and everything was unfair. She complained that her hair was not beautiful, her skin was too tan, she was dirty, and everyone was being mean to her.

After three days of being assaulted by an endless volley of Marguerite's verbal cannon balls, Thomas Stenhouse uncharacteristically retaliated. In a flash of fire and fury, he turned on his heels. Towering above her, Thomas' unshaven whiskers only inches from Marguerite's soft smooth face, he began to shout.

"Enough, young lady! I don't care that your ankles are bruised. I don't care that gathering mushrooms hurts your knees! And I don't care that you stink like a pig!" Thomas went on.

"I didn't say that I stink like a pig," she shouted in protest.

"WELL, YOU DO! And if I hear one more word from you, just one more complaint, I am going to take this here rope and hang you by your feet, young lady! I swear I will tie you upside down from one of these trees!" he shouted.

Marguerite's voice sputtered as she lost her earlier courage. She was too uncertain whether or not Thomas would really follow through with his threat. The anger in his eyes suggested that he might actually do it. Marguerite looked around the group for support, for someone to stand beside her. She thought Thomas was way out of line, addressing her as he was. Surely one of her brothers or friends would not allow such abuse to take place.

Thomas did not move. He continued to hoover above her, glaring down with his eyes just inches from hers. His bright red face glowing through his whiskers.

Marguerite took a step backward away from Thomas and turned dramatically around, making an effort to show everyone through her exaggerated movements just how thoroughly disgusted she was by his ungentlemanly actions.

She marched off the road toward the surrounding forest. As she scurried up a short hillside a few feet off the road, she slipped slightly and fell forward onto her hands. Those observing the scene below could not help but let out an unintentional bit of laughter. Feeling all the more upset and humiliated, she trounced over the top of the hill and down the other side into a shallow ravine.

Not even the Cardon or Pons girls had come to her rescue, which surprised James. Perhaps they too had grown weary of Marguerite. Or perhaps they were simply too afraid that Thomas would string them up by their feet as well. Either way, James was glad that someone had stood up to Marguerite, and gladder still that no one had come to her rescue.

After this event, Thomas led with more confidence. He was more certain in his ability to lead. Although he had been set apart as the presiding authority over their little band of travelers, it was not until this moment that he had truly claimed that role. It was also this event that earned him the respect of those that were assigned to follow him.

Marguerite's humiliation had an additional effect that James thought was equally beneficial. By not coming to her assistance, the Pons and Cardon girls had upset Marguerite. She believed that they had betrayed her, and as such, she refused to associate with any of them. Without any adoring fans, Marguerite no longer had an audience to impress. This, and the fact that she was now terrified of Thomas, resulted in a more subdued and quiet atmosphere.

Marguerite was still as unpleasant as before, but instead of acting like a lion that chased down its many victims, she now behaved more like a snake; her venom only being administered to those who wandered too close. And thus she remained the rest of the way to Paris.

1854

Chapter Seventeen

By Post and Packet

Paris was even more impressive than Geneva had been. Large spacious cathedrals topped by towering spires that rose up and almost out of sight. Beautiful estates with large manicured lawns, hedges, and rose gardens. Homes and shops as far as the eye could see.

Once again, the group was treated to a single night of good food and comfortable beds. And once again, everyone was in good spirits. Not just because their stomachs were full. But also because of the fact that London was now only three days away. And the journey between Paris and London would be done almost entirely by post and packet, requiring very little walking on their part.

From Paris, the sixty one Mormon converts were to travel by post to Calais, France. Traveling by post was an extremely costly privilege that was usually reserved only for upper class society. But due to the urgency of their schedule, their leaders had decided to make these more expensive arrangements.

James had never traveled so fast in his life. Their brisk speed tired the horses quickly. To keep the party moving as rapidly as possible, their carriages stopped every twenty to thirty miles so that the tired horses could be traded out for fresh animals. These stops lasted just long enough for the horses to be switched, and for everyone to take care of any personal needs, after which it was back to their breathtaking flight.

James could not help himself. He was mesmerized with excitement. Despite Jean and Antoinette telling him several times to get some sleep, James stayed awake most of the eighteen hour journey.

Once in Calais, the group boarded a couple of small packet ships. These specialized ships had been designed to cross the English Channel as fast as possible. Like the post carriages, they were also reserved for high priority mail, and passengers willing to pay the extra fare for the privilege of crossing the channel quickly.

For the next seven hours, James was treated to a ride that was even more thrilling than their journey across the countryside had been. Now they were not only moving quickly, but they were also bouncing up and down and from side to side. First, the ship would rise up so that James could not see the water ahead of them. Then it would come crashing downward with a great roaring thunder, sending salty water into the air in every direction. Once again, James was unable to sleep much. He did not want to miss a moment of the adventure.

Their ship arrived at the harbor of an English village that Thomas Stenhouse said was called Dover. Dover was somehow cleaner and seemed more refined than any of the cities they had yet passed through. The roads looked as though they had been frequently cared for and often repaired. Lining the streets were several gas powered lamps that provided light, even at night!

Almost the moment they arrived in Dover, the group once again boarded post carriages and set out for London. James had intended to also remain awake on this leg of their journey, but was quickly overcome by fatigue. Leaning onto Antoinette's shoulder,

James fell asleep about an hour into their ride. Where he remained asleep almost the entire eleven hours from Dover to London.

℘

As London rose over the hilltops in front of them, the sun began to rise on their right, casting its orange light across a sight that was surely too large to be a single city. Indeed, how could any city be that large? James could not imagine that there were enough people in the entire world to inhabit so many buildings. And yet inhabited they all seemed to be. Some of the streets they passed reminded James of home; the people were poor and dressed in rags. In their faces he saw that familiar look of hunger and need. Other streets were stunningly beautiful and opulent. Men and women walked along sidewalks dressed in outfits that to James seemed to be too fancy even for royalty.

Everywhere there were fancy carriages, fine horses, and beautiful homes. The streets were noisy. People were shouting, bells were ringing, animals were honking, and hundreds of other strange noises that James had never heard before rang out all around him.

The strangest thing to James, though, was how dirty everything was. Not like home, where James and his friends only ever got earth on them. This was different, and much worse. The buildings were covered with a depressing blackness. The streets had little streams that ran down them that smelled to James like an outhouse.

Even the sky was dirty. The familiar blue that James had grown up with was was there, but it was partially blotted out by black smoke which billowed out of endless chimneys as far as the eye could see.

It was a strange contrast. The people wore such fine clothing. Their carriages were meticulously cared for. Their horses and dogs so clean and manicured. And all of them were set in a place as filthy as any that James could imagine. It was odd to James that they wore such fine things in such a dreary place.

The travelers rode on for a long time, passing street after street. It took more than an hour of riding through London before they arrived at the Peacock Inn where they would spend the night.

This inn was not as nice as the two they had stayed in earlier in their trip. The beds were comfortable enough, but they were not as soft as they had been in Geneva. The food was edible and filling, but not as rich as it had been in Paris. James decided that he was just acting spoiled. The food may not be as good at the Peacock Inn as it had been in Paris, but it was still better than anything that he had eaten back home. And although the beds were not as comfortable as they had been in Geneva, at least he did not have to share a bed with his brothers.

The next morning was slower than they were used to. Instead of setting off at first light as they usually did, the group had to wait for Thomas Stenhouse to return. Thomas had gone to collect his family. He owned a small cottage just outside of London, and had spent most of his life here. Before the group could continue, Thomas needed to return home to his wife and children, who would be joining the group for the rest of the journey to Deseret.

Thomas' family had not seen him in more than four years. James imagined how happy they would be today, once they were together again. But how strange it must be for them to also have to leave their home and head for Deseret on the same day of their wonderful reunion. What faith they must have to first send their father away, and to then follow him into the American wilderness upon his return.

෨

Thomas felt more relaxed than he had in over two weeks. He was home! For at least a few moments he could pretend that everything was normal. He was not the leader of a band of pioneers. He had not been away from home for four years. And he was not about to leave London once again — forever.

No, he was just out for a stroll along the familiar streets that he had known his entire life. He was walking toward home where he would soon see his family. Of course, his fantasy would burst the moment he saw them.

Elizabeth would not have changed much in four years, but his sons, Micheal and Richard would be vastly different. Micheal will be ten years old and Richard six. They probably wouldn't even remember him. They certainly wouldn't recognize their father, nor was he likely to recognize them.

As Thomas made his way through the village streets and past the local butcher's market where he had often purchased meat for his little family, he once again considered the privilege that had been his to serve the Lord. Like Paul of old, Thomas had been called of God to travel to distant lands to preach the gospel. He had gone with little money and with a heart full of faith that the Lord would help him eat and provide a place to sleep each night. Leaving Elizabeth and his sons behind had been difficult, but it was a small price to pay, thought Thomas. Look at what has come about as a result of the sacrifices made by the missionaries who served in Italy and Switzerland. Sixty Saints were traveling with faith from their homelands in Europe to the Promised Land in America. And these sixty were only the first group. Others would follow.

True their missions had not produced the thousands of converts John Taylor's mission to England had, but every soul was just as precious.

∞

James and most of his family spent the morning wandering through some of the shops that were close to their inn. They did not dare wander too far, both out of a fear of getting lost, and also out of concern that they would miss the return of Thomas. Besides, they did not have any money to spend in these shops anyway. However, they still enjoyed looking at all of the various oddities from around the world. Shelves full of pristine books, beautifully handcrafted shoes, dolls from distant lands, paintings, fine plates, and silverware.

In one shop, the local children looked to be enjoying what Jean called "sweets." There were ribbons of gooey-looking color laid out on sheets of paper, brown dabs of something that came from the Americas called "chocolate," and a variety of other treats. James' impoverished state kept him from learning if they tasted as good as they smelled.

After leaving the sweetshop, they decided they had better head back to the inn. The morning was growing late, and they did not want to keep the group waiting. Thomas would likely be back soon, if he wasn't already.

The four Waldensian vagabonds walked side by side, taking up the entire sidewalk. James supposed that they must have been quite a sight! Four dirty foreigners, wearing worn out clothing, unable to understand a single word that anyone spoke to them.

As they slowly made their way toward the inn, a beautifully dressed, but wrinkly, unkind, and irritated looking woman approached them. Looking at Jean, who was the tallest of the four, she said several things that none of them understood. Her voice was loud and disdainful. After addressing Jean, she pushed through the group and continued along her way, likely not realizing that none of them had the slightest idea what she had said.

Antoinette looked at Jean and smiled. Both of them then began to laugh. "She was upset with you, Jean," admonished Antoinette. "You mustn't do . . . whatever it is you were doing, young man," she said in mock scolding.

"Yes, yes, chap," interrupted a very dirty and scruffy looking Daniel. "This is England, my good man. We must behave like Gentleman."

ℰ

There is something very wonderful about walking through your own neighborhood. It is a great comfort to see the buildings that you have known since your days as a young boy still standing tall and strong. Each of the trees right where they are supposed to be. Perhaps a little taller, but not out of place. The sounds and smells exactly as you left them. The same old man sitting outside the same old shop, just as he has done for as long as you can remember.

Thomas began to quicken his pace as he came to the last hill that obscured the view of his dear home. A few more steps and he would see it. The cottage that he had grown up in, and that he had inherited from his father when he died ten years earlier. The home where he had planned to raise his own children. It was not large, but it was comfortable. Made from the finest wood, and painted blue and white. It may not have been a palace, but to Thomas it was better than any castle, because it was his.

The bottom story had a small kitchen, a drawing room, and a dining room. The upper floor had three bedrooms. It was just the right size for him, his wife and their boys. It was perfect in every way.

Thomas opened the gate that separated his yard from the street and headed toward the front door. As he entered his home, he was impressed with the sameness that it bore to how he had left it. Not a single nicknack was out of place. It was strange to think that they would be leaving it all behind. The home and all its contents would become the property of his younger brother Theodore. He and his family would now live here, while Thomas, his wife, and their two children headed off into the unknown

American frontier.

"Thomas, is that you?" he heard Elizabeth calling from the kitchen. She sounded like an angel.

"Oh, my dear Thomas!" she proclaimed as she came bursting through the door. They embraced as Elizabeth cried on Thomas' coat. Thomas also shed tears of joy as he held his dear companion close to him.

"Come here, boys," Elizabeth called, still holding Thomas. "Come greet your father."

Thomas had never seen two more handsome boys. They were dressed in their finest clothing, and in their faces they looked just as beautiful as their mother.

"Say hello," encouraged Elizabeth.

"Hello, Father," Micheal, the older of the two said shyly.

"Hello," copied Richard, even quieter than Micheal had.

"Let's all sit down, I have been cooking all morning for you, my dear," said Elizabeth. "I made all the things you used to love. Before we leave our home, let's enjoy one last meal here together," she said, clearly doing her best not to let her emotions betray her sadness in leaving her home behind.

In a voice that resounded with courage, she ushered the family into the dining room where she had set the table using the family's finest dishes and silverware. Together, the Stenhouse family ate a meal fit for a king. There was more food than any of them could have eaten, even if they had had a week to accomplish the task.

When they were all full and utterly satisfied by the delicious meal, Thomas helped Elizabeth clean up. And then, after being home for only an hour, they walked toward the front door. Each of them picked up a duffel bag that Elizabeth had packed for them, and after looking around one last time, they walked out. Never again would any of them see their beautiful home.

8)

The road from London to Liverpool took another week to travel and consisted of a mixture of walking and carriage rides. It seemed to James that England was a strangely tame place, almost like Mother Nature herself had been subjected to the authority of the English King. The countryside, of course, still had its fair share of wild places. But everywhere one looked there were reminders that you were in the most powerful empire on Earth. Military regiments passed them on the well maintained roads. They frequently passed cottages with beautiful gardens. Road signs were scattered about, pointing to distant villages, with descriptions that told weary travelers how far away a particular place was.

James had the feeling that the English had not only conquered the people of the world, but that they had also mastered the elements.

1854

Chapter Eighteen

A Multitude of Saints

The tired group of Waldensian and Swiss Mormons arrived in Liverpool, England, on March 10, 1854. Just two days before their ship was scheduled to leave port for America, and thirty three days after James and his family had left the safety of their home, and the arms of their Papa.

Arriving safely in Liverpool greatly lifted the spirits of almost all of the road-weary travelers. No one had been lost. No one had been injured, or fallen ill. If they could cross the European continent safely, then surely they could also cross the American continent. How much more difficult could that land be?

The port in Liverpool was a busy and impressive place. Everywhere men were shouting orders, lifting boxes, and driving wagons. Ropes could be seen working their way like spider webs across the many ships and shore rafters. James and his family were each assigned a bed in the lower deck of the sailing vessel called the John M. Wood. Here they would sleep the next two nights, awaiting their departure for America, and then the next several weeks after that as they crossed the high seas.

There was no privacy. Their bunks were built into the ship, alongside hundreds of others. They would be sleeping in the open room where any of the more than eight hundred other passengers could see them.

Thomas Stenhouse introduced James and his family to Robert Campbell. He would be acting as their leader for the remainder of their journey. Brother Campbell only spoke English, making communicating with him difficult. The sixty one Waldensian and Swiss converts now joined a vast throng of Mormons known as the 74th Company of Saints, which totaled three hundred and ninety seven individuals, all of them huddled in the same part of the ship. Everywhere people were reading the Book of Mormon, saying prayers, and worshiping together.

Everyone looked dirty and tired. James supposed that like his family, they had each left their homes and traveled across Europe in answer to the call of a living prophet. So many different languages and traditions united by a common gospel message. James did not need to speak their languages to share a bond with them. They were Saints, traveling together toward the Promised Land.

They were not entirely confined to the ship. During the day, they could explore Liverpool, walk through shops, or sit along the shore and watch the many ships come and go.

But as novel as it was to experience the many different aspects that Liverpool had to offer, James was eager to begin the next part of their adventure toward Deseret. They had already crossed one continent, they could certainly handle another. The next two months would be spent sailing on a ship. They wouldn't have to do any walking at all. James looked forward to what he supposed would be a perfect holiday.

Appendix

The Actual Letter Written By Elder Lorenzo Snow of The Quorum of The Twelve Apostles To President Orson Hyde, President of The Quorum of The Twelve Apostles

Dear President Hyde,

After seven months residence in Italy, I am going to bid it farewell for a season. If the attractions of physical nature could command all my attention, I might long linger to gaze upon these realms of loveliness. One might travel far over the earth before he finds a fairer clime. Here man dwells beneath an almost cloudless sky. The sun scarcely hides his face in summer or winter; and when, at eventide, his golden glories fade behind the western hills, the silver stars shed a serene lustre over the blue vault of immensity. But, the remembrance of the moral scenery amid which I have been moving will be more imperishably engraved on my spirit, than all the brightness of the firmament, or the verdure of prairies enamelled with ten thousand flowers. Amid the loveliness of nature I found the soul of man like a wilderness. From the palace of the King, to the lone cottage on the mountain, all was shrouded in spiritual darkness. Protestant and Papist looked upon each other as outcasts from the hopes of eternity; but regarded themselves as the favorites of heaven. And thus they had done from time immemorial. The changing ephemeral sectarianism of England and

America, is, in many respects, unlike the sturdy superstition of this country. Here, Protestantism is not the offspring of boasted modern reformation; but may fairly dispute with Rome as to which is the oldest in apostacy. Every man holds a creed which has been transmitted from sire to son for a thousand years, whether he be Protestant or Catholic; and often he will lay his hand on his heart, and swear by the faith of his forefathers, that he will live, and die, as they have lived and died.

The Protestants form a very small minority. They have been harassed for centuries by fierce attacks from powerful armies of Catholics; but after sanguinary persecutions, they have revived as the corn, and grown as the vine. Once their last remnant was driven to Switzerland; but a courageous minister, assuming a military character, led them back victoriously to their native valleys. The portrait of this hero bears the following inscription:--

"I preach and fight; I have a double commission; and these two contests occupy my soul. Zion is now to be rebuilt, and the sword is needed as well as the trowel."

The English government has several times interfered in their behalf; and large donations have been sent them from various Protestant countries. Many a tribute of admiration has been paid them by men of ability from the chief sects of Protestantism, till their little church has been flattered into immeasurable self-importance.

The following hymn expresses the feelings engendered by their romantic situation:--

For the strength of the hills we bless thee,
    Our God, our fathers' God;
    Thou hast made thy children mighty
    By the touch of the mountain sod.
    Thou hast fixed our ark of refuge
    Where the spoiler's foot ne'er trod.
    For the strength of the hills we bless thee,
    Our God, our fathers' God.
  We are watchers of a beacon
    Whose light must never die;

We are guardians of an altar
  'Midst the silence of the sky.
The rocks yield founts of courage,
  Struck forth as by Thy rod;
For the strength of the hills we bless thee,
  Our God, our fathers' God.

For the dark resounding caverns,
  Where Thy still, small voice is heard;
For the strong pines of the forests,
  That by Thy breath are stirred;
For the storm, on whose free pinions,
  Thy spirit walks abroad;
For the strength of the hills we bless thee,
  Our God, our fathers' God.

The royal eagle darteth
  O'er his quarry from the heights,
And the stag, that knows no master,
  Seeks there his wild delights;
But we, for Thy communion,
  Have sought the mountain sod.
For the strength of the hills we bless thee,
  Our God, our fathers' God.

The banner of the chieftain,
  Far, far below us waves;
The war-horses of the spearman
  Cannot reach our lofty caves.
Thy dark clouds wrapt the threshold
  Of freedom's last abode.
For the strength of the hills we bless thee,
  Our God, our fathers' God.

For the shadow of Thy presence
  Round our camp of rock outspread;
For the stern defiles of battle,

Bearing record of our dead;
For the snows and for the torrents,
  For the free heart's burial sod;
For the strength of the hills we bless thee,
  Our God, our fathers' God.

Their self-esteem, joined with deep ignorance, presents a formidable opposition to the progress of the Gospel. They have had so little intercourse with other parts of the earth--so little knowledge of any thing beyond their own scenes of pastoral life, that it is difficult for them to contemplate the great principles of temporal and eternal salvation.

One long round of almost unremitting toil is the portion of both sexes. The woman who is venerable with grey hairs is seen laden with wood, or heavy baskets of manure, while travelling the rugged paths of the mountains. No drudgery here but what must be shared by the delicate female frame. I have travelled far over the earth, from the confines of the torrid Zone to the regions of eternal snow, but never before beheld a people with so many mental and physical derangements. But the hour of their deliverance draws nigh.

The constitution of this kingdom affords no guarantee that we shall ever enjoy the same religious privileges as our brethren in England and other countries.

A merciful providence has hitherto preserved us from being entangled in the meshes of the law. A bookseller told me, the other day, that he was not allowed to sell a Bible. No work is permitted to be published that attacks the principles of Catholicism. I look with wonder upon the road by which the Lord hath led me since I came to this land. From the first day that I trod the Italian soil, there has been a chain of circumstances which has not sprung from chance, but from the wise arrangements of Him who ruleth in the kingdoms of men. I thank my Heavenly Father that I was restrained from any attempt to hurry the great work with which I was entrusted. All the jealous policy of Italy has been hushed into repose by the comparative silence of our operations; and, at the same time, no principle has been compromised, no concession has been made, but from day to day, we were always engaged forming some new acquaintance, or breaking down some ancient barrier of prejudice.

Such slowness was not agreeable to me as a man; but I look forward to the day when the stability and grandeur of our building will be an ample reward for those months of labour which may not have been attended with any thing extraordinary in the eyes of those who judge merely by the external appearance of the moment.

Here I may relate a dream, which though simple in itself, presented a theme for meditation under our peculiar circumstances.

I thought I was in company with some friends, descending a gentle slope of beautiful green, till we came to the bank of a large body of water. Here were two skiffs; and as I embarked in the one, my friends followed in the other. we moved slowly over the face of the wide-spreading bay, without wind, or any exertion on our part. As we were on a fishing excursion, we were delighted to behold large and beautiful fish on the surface of the water, all around, to a vast distance. we beheld many persons spreading their nets and lines; but they seemed to be all stationary; whereas, we were in continual motion. While passing one of them, I discovered a fish had got upon my hook, and I thought it might, perhaps, disturb this man's feelings to have it caught, as it were, out of his hands; nevertheless, we moved along, and came to the shore. I then drew in my line, and was not a little surprised and mortified as the smallness of my prize. I thought it very strange that, among such a vast multitude of noble, superior-looking fish, I should have made so small a haul. But all my disappointments vanished when I came to discover that its qualities were of a very extraordinary character.

While encircled by many persons of noble bearing and considerable intelligence, a prospect seemed opening for the employment of some among them in the work of the ministry. but the Lord judgeth not as man judgeth. The first native of these valleys that I ordained to preach the Gospel was one who swayed no extended influence, and boasted no great natural abilities; but he sought the Lord with fasting and prayer, and the Spirit began to rest upon him mightily, showing him, in the dreams of night, the glorious reality of that work with which he had become associated.

Feeling it wisdom to send Elder Stenhouse to Switzerland, and to leave Elder Woodard in Italy; and knowing the formidable character of the difficulties with which they must struggle, I resolved to bestow upon them such blessings as they required to the discharge of their important duties; and as there is power, knowledge, and wisdom in the High Priesthood, I felt it was according to the mind of the Spirit that they should be called to that office.

We have here no temple--no building made of human hands, but the mountain's tower around us, far above all the edifices which Protestants or Papists use in this country. On Sunday, the 24th of November, we ascended one of these eminences which seem to occupy a position between earth and sky, and which, on a former occasion, we had named Mount Brigham. During our tedious ascent, the sun shone forth in its brightness; but in such parts as were shaded, we found snow upon the ground, and many a craggy peak and rocky summit on every side was white with fleeces of winter. Having reached the spot we sought, we gazed with rapture on the enchanting scenes of surrounding nature. Before us was a plain so vast, that it seemed as if immensity had become visible. All was level in this ocean of space, and yet no sameness appeared on its fertile bosom. Here towns and cities were environed by the resources from which their inhabitants had been fed for ages. Ancient and far-famed Italy, the scene of our mission, was spread out like a vision before our enchanted eyes. Light and shade produced their effect in that vast picture to a surprising degree; for while the clouds flung their shadows on one part, another was illuminated with the most brilliant sun-light, as far as the eye could reach. but there was one hallowing reflection which threw all around a brighter lustre than the noon-tide firmament: it was in that place, two months before, that we organized the Church of Jesus Christ in Italy. If we had stood upon a pavement of gold and diamonds, it would not have produced an impression like the imperishable remembrance of that sacred scene.

Amid this sublime display of the Creator's works, we sung the praises of His eternal Name, and implored those gifts which our circumstances required.

I then ordained Elder Woodard as a High Priest, and asked my Heavenly Father to give him wisdom and strength to watch over the Church in Italy, whatever might be the scenes through which it should have to pass, and that he might be enabled to extend the work which I had commenced. I also ordained Elder Stenhouse as a High Priest, and prayed that his way might be opened in Switzerland for carrying forth the work of the Lord in that interesting country.

The Mountain Christians: For The Strength of The Hills

In a few days afterwards, Elder Stenhouse proceeded on his mission.

O Italy! thou birth-place and burial-ground of the proud Caesars, who swayedst the sceptre of this mundane creating--land of literature and arts, and once the centre of the world's civilization--who shall tell all the greatness which breathes in the story of thy past? and who, oh! who shall tell all the corruption which broods on thy bosom NOW?

Land of flowers and fruitfulness of the vine, the olive and orange, all that blushes in beauty and charms with delicacy is spread o'er thy green fields, or grows in thy empire garden; but they children are deep in pollution, and spring like thorns and thistles, amid thy floral scenes of endless enchantment. From the wave-swept shores of the Mediterranean to the base of the bleak Alpine region, thy sunny plains lie spread like a fairy realm. Here reposes the dust of millions that were mighty in ages gone by, and flooded the earth with the fame of their deeds. Here are the fields that have been crimsoned with the blood of royalty, and have become the grave of dynasties. Poets that sung for the praises of nations, and princes that wielded the Sceptre of power during many a crisis of the world's history, are laid low beneath the dust of thy fields and vineyards.

But is there nought here save the tomb or the past? O, Italy! hath an eternal winter followed the summer of thy fame, and frosted the flowers of thy genius, and clouded the sun-beams of glory? No! the future of thy story shall outshine the past, and thy children shall yet be more renowned than in the ages of old. Though the triple crown of earth's proudest apostate shed a tinsel splendour over thy boundless superstition, Truth shall yet be victorious amid thy Babylonish regions. Where triumphant warriors were stained with gore, and princes reigned in the pomp of tyranny, the sure, though tardy working of the Gospel now weaves a fairer wreath, and wins a brighter crown. i see around me many an eye which will, one day, glisten with delight at the tidings of Eternal Truth--many a countenanced which will adorn the assemblies of the Living God. There is yet the blood of heaven's nobility within the hearts of many amid thy sons and daughters; and sooner will that blood stain the scaffold of martyrdom, than dishonour the manly spirits with which it is connected.

Geneva, February 6th.--I have reserved the closing of my letter till my arrival in Geneva. As I took my departure from Piedmont, much kindly feeling was manifested towards me. I beheld, with no small degree of satisfaction, the work of the Lord extending, and the lively efforts in operation for the spread of the principles of Truth. You may form some idea of the difficulties which have beset my efforts to publish, when I tell you that "The Voice of Joseph" is now circulating in Italy, with a woodcut of a CATHOLIC NUN, ANCHOR, LAMP, and CROSS on the first page, and on the last, NOAH'S ARK, the DOVE, and the OLIVE. With this work, and "The Ancient Gospel Restored," in my trunk, pockets, and hat I crossed the Alps, in the midst of a storm of snow, scarcely knowing whether I was dead or alive. It is one thing to read of travelling over the back bone of Europe in the depth of winter; but doing it is quite different.

Since my arrival in the famed city of Calvin, I have had several interviews with some intelligent Swill gentlemen, who have, through the efforts of Elder Stenhouse, and the circulation of my works, becomes much interested, and promise fair to give a good investigation to the work. In consequence of so much difficulty and vexation in getting out publications in Italy, I feel unwilling to draw many books from that quarter; therefore, I feel it my duty to make arrangements to get published, here, a second edition of both works. I am much pleased with the prospect of establishing the Gospel in Geneva. I feel FREE, and in a FREE atmosphere and to prophecy GOOD OF SWITZERLAND.

Yours affectionately,
LORENZO SNOW

To President Orson Hyde,
President of The Quorum of The Twelve Apostles
    Kanesville, Iowa Territory,
      North America

Appendix II

On The Origin of The Waldensian People

There is much debate among modern-day scholars regarding the origin of the Waldensians. The most commonly held view today is that they originated in 1176 and that they were followers of a man named Peter Waldo. Another theory is that the Waldensian movement began at the end of the Seventh Century with Bishop Claudius of Turin who objected to the worship of idols that he believed was entering into the Catholic Church. The third, and final theory is that they began in the days of Jesus Christ, and that they never joined themselves to the body of the Catholic Church.

I chose to write this book from that latter perspective, because this is what James himself would have been taught. In 1853, it was commonly accepted and taught by the Waldensians that they originated in the days of Christ. They believed that they had never united themselves with the Catholic Church, but had instead hid away in the mountains an entirely different faith since their founding.

It is clear from studying the writings of Lorenzo Snow that he shared this view. Additionally, there are certain clues in the piedmontese language that hint at an earlier origin than 800 AD. Also, within the libraries of the Vatican there are references to this people that seem to predate 800 AD.

There is no way to definitely say one way or the other where this people really came from. The only thing that we can be certain of is that by 1176 the

Waldensians were well established and thriving in their mountains.

The Author's own feelings are that this faith began in the days of Christ. However, I have no evidence to support this view. It is simply a romantic way for it to have begun.

I do however feel that it was important to write the story from the perspective that James himself would have had, which is that the heritage of his people extended back all the way to Christ and his Apostles.

The Mountain Christians

More Books In This Series

www.MountainChristians.com

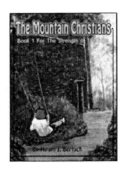

Volume One:

For The Strength of The Hills

Published 2012

Volume Two:

Master, The Tempest Is Raging

Volume Three:

Shall The Youth of Zion Falter

Volume Four:

Firm As The Mountains Around Us

Sign Up At Our Website To Be Notified

of Specific Release Dates

www.MountainChristians.com

The Mountain Christians

Please Review This Book Online & Win Prizes For Doing So

We depend upon online book reviews. Your reviews helps others discover this book. We ask that you please take a moment and write an honest & unbiased review in one or more of the many online book resources. **Whether you enjoyed our book or not, please tell others what you thought!**

Win Prizes For Leaving A Review

Visit www.MountainChristians.com/win-prizes-lds-novel.php to learn how you can win prizes for your non-biased reviews. Winners will be selected from among those who leave reviews, who like our facebook page, tweet about our book, add this book to their Goodreads.com Profile, or otherwise help to spread the word about The Mountain Christians. **Whether you make positive or negative comments or reviews, you can enter to win.**

Scan QR Code To Win Prizes

About The Author

Hiram Bertoch

Hiram Bertoch lives in Hunter, Utah with his wife Anna and their seven children. As a family, they care for a small farm that their family has operated for seven generations.

Hiram began his career teaching in the Jordan and Granite School Districts. In 1998 he founded The KidsKnowIt Network (www.kidsknowit.com), which today is among the most popular educational resources for children on the Internet. Serving some 350 million children worldwide.

Hiram has served on various boards, and in leadership positions for other companies and organizations.

Hiram serves as both the President of The Board of Trustees, and also as the Sexton for the Pleasant Green Cemetery, an historic pioneer cemetery in the Oquirrh Mountains, overlooking the Salt Lake Valley.

Hiram enjoys writing and does so between other projects. Usually either on his tablet, or on his cellphone using Swype. Much of this book was written in this manner, while waiting between appointments and other obligations.

CPSIA information can be obtained at www.ICGtesting.com
Printed in the USA
BVOW010152201212

308669BV00005B/14/P